Praise for
Robert Ward's First Novel,
SHEDDING SKIN

"*SHEDDING SKIN* [is] a novel in overdrive—vulgar, outrageous, totally hyperbolic, exceptionally funny, and written with an uncommon attention to the wonders of language. . . . Robert Ward [is] a writer to remember and envy. . . ."
>—Sheldon Frank, *The New York Times Book Review*

"I loved this book. . . . *Easy Rider* meets *Catcher in the Rye*. Bob Ward is the J.D. Salinger of rock 'n' roll."
>—Tony Hendra, author of *The Book of Bad Virtues*

"O sages of Baltimore! Burning in a bright fire! O Sidney Lanier, E.A. Poe, H.L. Mencken, V.F. Calverton, Frank Zappa, John Barth! Welcome Robert Ward to your midst. . . . [A] remarkable first novel. . . . Funny, lyric. . . . The pace is relentless. . . . A smile, slashed with a razor's edge. . . . The manic strength of the novel lies in Ward's ability to set fascinating characters loose on the page. . . . Read *SHEDDING SKIN*."
>—*Baltimore Sun*

"I read *SHEDDING SKIN* years ago and still wake up sometimes thinking about it. Few books I've read last so long in memory or deserve to."
>—James Whitehead, author of *Joiner*

"Startlingly original. . . . A very funny novel which offers genuine insight—for a change—into the youth scene. . . . Ward is a connoisseur of the Sixties. . . . Robert Ward writes beautifully, and *SHEDDING SKIN* augurs a brilliant future for him as a novelist."
>—Lee Seay, *The Nashville Banner*

Books by Robert Ward

The Cactus Garden
The King of Cards
Red Baker
Cattle Annie and Little Britches
Shedding Skin

Shedding Skin

Robert Ward

WASHINGTON SQUARE PRESS
PUBLISHED BY POCKET BOOKS

New York   London   Toronto   Sydney   Tokyo   Singapore

"In Which the Narrator Becomes a Mountain Man and Harvests the Grapes of Wrath" and "In Which the Narrator Meets the Phantom of Cleveland and Learns That There Is No Business Like Show Business" originally appeared in *The Carolina Quarterly,* Fall 1969.

"A Priest for My Parents," "Art and Celery," and "The End of Innocence and All That" originally appeared in *The Carolina Quarterly,* Fall 1971.

"In Which the Narrator Becomes a Mountain Man and Harvests the Grapes of Wrath" appeared in *Works in Progress,* Number 4, © 1971 by The Literary Guild of America, Inc.

"The Terror of the Swami and Some Speed-Freak Football" originally appeared in the *Seneca Review,* November 30, 1971.

A Washington Square Press Publication of
POCKET BOOKS, a division of Simon & Schuster Inc.
1230 Avenue of the Americas, New York, NY 10020

Copyright © 1972 by Robert Ward

ISBN: 0-671-53613-3

First Washington Square Press trade paperback printing
October 1995

10 9 8 7 6 5 4 3 2 1

WASHINGTON SQUARE PRESS and colophon are registered trademarks of Simon & Schuster Inc.

Cover design by Matt Galemmo. Cover photo credits: top, © Henri Carter-Bresson/Magnum Photos, Inc.; bottom, Daniel O'Connell

Printed in the U.S.A.

This book is dedicated to:
Ray Franke
Mike Disend
Bill Harrison
Jack Hicks

PART ONE

I.

In Which I Begin by Digging My Hole

I have my blue jeans rolled up to reveal the plaid underside and my Tom Corbett Space Cadet T-shirt clings tight to my stomach. Yes, and my white high-topped Keds surround my dancing feet, my red bandanna is tied around my neck, the point tickling my throat. Behind me, in the row house, Freda and Father sit beneath the Norman Rockwell kitchen calendar arguing about budgets. Ahead of me is Craig Avenue. That's where the Hill is, where Baba Looie might be. It is where Gene Autry and Roy Rogers move inside our bodies, take over our speech, stop stuttering in Walter, make Kirk forget his scraped-up knees, turn Shirley Steinberg—who will later get gunned down for real in a tavern fight—into the traveling minstrel girl, charm a man out of his snake ring like it or not. Running down Craig Avenue, I'm no fat kid who will have trouble with braces acne marriage. I will not step on a crack. I am Lash LaRue; the bushes shrink from my touch. Me and

3

my silver gun, my jewel-studded holster. Even though I cannot breathe with this scarf strangling my neck. I can still dodge Walter's bullet.

"Gotcha!"

"Missed."

"Didn't. Can't dodge two feet."

"Can, Walter. Jump the exact moment you pull the trigger. Before the bullet comes out of the gun, I'm free."

"Sure."

A punch in the gut for Walt. See him lying on the chalked hopscotch, his head resting in sevensies. Kirk from the mulberry tree:

"Krehhh, krehhhh, you're all dead."

No chance to dodge. Call in the rulebook.

"Fix fix new man."

"No new men. No new men. Awwww no."

I may as well die, change the game to Best Death.

No one wants to play. It doesn't matter. We go to the Hill. Dust all over Tom Corbett's shirt. Standing on the Hill, should we go get the Seckel pears? No, Greenleaf will call the cops. *What's a penny made of? Dirty copper. So funny I forgot to laugh.* Later we will say *Funny as a fart in a space suit.*

"Let's dig."

Run over to Walter's for the shovel. Little Eddie, who has painted valentines on the backs of his box turtles, wants to dig. We push him out of the way. No one likes him because he has a cleft palate. Dig dig dig, working good here in the sunshine, dirt all over Kirk like moondust, digging further into that soft orange clay, stop, wipe off your head with the bandanna, go over to Eddie's—yes, you can play, we love you, bring us the water bottle, bring us the ruler with the King Syrup picture on it; we've got a nice hole here now, three feet deep. Sweat all over us, as we sit in the hole, lob grenades at Japs, slitty-eyed midgets never stop Combat Kelly or the Blackhawks. Shoot marbles against the wall, get all the way down, we could store apples in here, Greenleaf comes looking, we spread a dark army blanket overtop and he breaks his leg. Dust all over everything, it's four o'clock, time for Kate Smith, do you wanna go? No, nah, forget it, she's a horse, never wears anything but long dresses because her calves are burned, nothing but scars. You wanna dig? *Yeah yeah yeah.* Let's get this hole deeper, all the way to China. I wanna buy some chop suey, digging digging, our hands coated with the dust, our shovels cracking into rock, digging digging digging our hole. . . .

II.

The Town of Thatched Rooves

There are Glenn and Freda, my parents, locked behind the shiny bathroom door, him screaming as she lances his pustules, and here am I in my room, eating Toll House cookies, playing with my battery of imaginary friends in the Town of Thatched Rooves. A warm town with kettles of stew, and big bulky men with red noses and orange weather-chapped cheeks. A town like Dickens' England, and all of them love me. Yes, I am in the pub, sitting behind the great oaken table, smiling and pounding my fist. Swans sail through every leaded window and even though most of the men are bloodthirsty pirates, they refuse to bother the swans in deference to me, their young but able-bodied leader.

"Hey, mates, how's 'bout another round o' ale?"

"Why not, Pete, why the hell not?"

All our arms are around one another, and we're singing with full-bodied bass voices about the good ship *Elizabeth*, and eye-patches are being snapped into place, capes swirling through blue fog air. Behind me someone is tapping his wolf's-head cane on the sawdust floor with resounding thumps. And I, Bobby Ward, am full, full, warm all over. . . .

"We got it, Bobby, we got it."

In the narrow hallway, my father's eyes are popping out of his forehead. Yellow light blocking out Mother's face, as she screeches like a wounded cricket.

"We got the bastard, the big one on his back. We got it."

My father turns around to reveal the sliced cyst. Blood and pus run down his back, seep over the edge of the flower-printed towel wrapped wrinkly around his waist.

"You see," says my mother. "He just leans forward and we get the maximum amount of pressure on it. Then all we need to do is flick it with the lance and booooom! It explodes."

My father's mouth is hanging open, and he is shaking his head like an epileptic.

"We really got the son of a bitch. Yessiree bob. Son a bitch only responds to one thing—*Force force and more force* —'n' 'at's jest what we gave it you better believe it."

I tell him that I do certainly believe it and slam the door. Then I sit staring at my cowboy curtains, looking at Roy and Dale, Trigger, Pat Brady and his jeep, Nellybell, waiting for them to move, to take me to Bobby Benson's B-Bar-B Ranch, where we will shoot and fight and be in the real.

But tonight it doesn't happen. I am aware of the curtains as cloth, and I am aware of the stitches which make up Roy's slant eyes. Even Nellybell is not 3-D, or metal, but flat, very flat, small black stitches in cotton. I climb out of bed and sit by my window.

"This is no way to grow up," I tell my imaginary friend Warren. "This is liable to do very bad things to my consciousness. I am liable to become demented."

7

"That's true," says Warren. "You are probably going to be a neurotic, audacious brat who is brilliant in short spurts but who is too fragmented to be decent."

"Gee," I sob. "Is there no chance for me?"

"None."

Warren's voice is the voice of the aristocrat who has just turned down the peasants' request for land reforms. I picture myself reaching down my own throat, grabbing him by his short legs and pulling him out of my body. But I do not do that for fear that he will be a small replica of myself.

"Ah, you might make it anyway," he says, without conviction.

"Thanks," I say. Then I let him sweep me away from Roy and Dale (who are still not Roy and Dale but only stitches), across the cold floor. And not a moment too soon, for blue lightning is crossing the room. Gray smoke is circling my head. From the other side of the wall my father makes a cry of pained delight. I shut my eyes and feel Warren turn over in my stomach. He is going to sleep now. I assume that it is time for me to do the same.

III.
A Priest for My Parents

My father and I are out in the alley. He has read a book which tells you How to Be a Pal to Your Son, and he is throwing me this ball.

"Good catch, Bobby."

I throw him a curve and it hits the chest. He begins to scream:

"You're trying to hurt my chest. You know I have that new bump there and you're trying to smash it. If you keep it up, I'm going to quit."

"Sorry, Dad."

He throws me the ball with a girlish flip. I watch the pigeons land on the telephone wires and I wish I could go with them to Capistrano. I am throwing slowly now, standing in the middle of the alley. Actually, I'm back in the pub with Errol Flynn; Wallace Beery is in the background adjusting his eyepatch and my father is throwing me the pinkie again.

9

"What do you want to do this year in school?"

"I want to do very good."

"That's wonderful, and what subjects do you like?"

"I love all my subjects, Da-Da."

He is standing at the other end of the alley, his hands on his hips.

"You're mocking me. You shouldn't do that. I'll not stand for it."

I am surprised to hear him say "I'll not stand for it." That's a favorite of Mother Freda's. In fact, so is standing with the hands on the hips. I think my father is slowly becoming the same person as my mother.

"Your father's identity is on shaky grounds," says Warren.

"How will I come out of this crisis?"

"To you the damage is already done."

"But how?"

"You'll see later."

"Warren, you are a drag."

I throw my father a fast ball and it hits him on one of his forehead gacks.

"Christ, oh Christ. Oh me. Oh no Christ."

My father is hopping around at the other end of the alley, his eighty-nine-cent vinyl glove dangling from his wrist.

"My forehead. Oh my forehead. You've done this, you little bastard."

I throw my own glove next to the rusting American Flyer bike which is lying in the backyard crabgrass and go up the rotting steps to the kitchen. Inside, my mother is talking to herself.

"I was such a nice innocent girl. I was so sweet. Why? Why?"

"When was this?" I ask her.

"This was before you were born."

"Why aren't you happy now, Mother? Can't you be sweet and innocent again?"

"What do you mean, again?" she screams, bunching her cheeks together like a fist. "I am still basically sweet and innocent. Underneath. It's underneath."

She stares at me. Her great, broad face, the left eye twitching madly. I want to help her. But the words don't come out that way.

"Why don't you go get a new boyfriend?"

She gasps, runs her fist across her lips.

"Oh God, to think I raised a beast. To think of the nights I sat up when you were sick."

I picture her swaying my rocker. I remember her telling me how she warded off rats when we lived in Washington. I am flooded with deep guilt and want to slice off my tongue. I hug her tightly, hoping that I may somehow squeeze the innocence from within, make it appear on her skin, light up her eyes.

"I could have married Ronald Hogan," she says.

"The missionary?" I ask.

"Yes, the missionary," she says, sniffling back the tears. "That's the very one. I had many a chance. The boys would come over and we'd make homemade ice cream and sing songs. Ronald was a tall, pale boy, not anywhere near as handsome as your father, but he knew something your father will never know."

"What's that?" I say on cue.

"He knew how to . . ."

"Be kind."

The voice is my father's. He's come from the alley, still holding his chest.

"That supercilious idiot," he says. "Yes, it's a damn shame you didn't marry him. I can see you both now in the remotest outpost of the Dark Continent. You and Ronald Hogan. He armed with the Old Testament and you with your innocence. Yes, your great, beautiful innocence. Like a protective shield you see on TV."

My mother is in tears. For a moment I feel a great loathing for my father. I want to butt him with my head. Then my mother leaps up and runs down into the cellar. My father sits in her place. He puts his head in his hands. Rocks back and forth.

"I'm sorry about hitting you with the ball," I say.

"I could have married the missionary," he says through his nose.

He begins to chuckle. Though I don't think it that funny, I chuckle mightily. The only time we are united is when I assent to his bitterness.

IV.
Mother Freda Turns into the Heap

Mother Freda's existence is a song with a single stanza. Endless repetitions of that one line, accompanied by a dull, persistent drumming which allows for no variations. Only exhaustion accounts for the occasional pauses in her imbecilic tune, pauses which introduce, for the briefest of moments, a new melody, equally as banal as the first.

This month she is blowing all the chords she knows to the Symphony of Participation. Ashley Montagu (pronounced Managooo) and Margaret Mead have stirred her into swirling whirlwinds of activity. She bursts into my room in her massive green artist's smock, proclaiming self-realization. She stands on one blubbery leg, waving her arms like windmills from the Town of Thatched Rooves. Of course, she should have seen *it* years ago. How could *it* have ever escaped her? Do I realize that in Georgia Maine Kansas Alaska women past forty are shaking the world? I do not. And if they, then why not she?

Is life (I ask you) a wall, built on dedication to family alone? It is *not*. It is more like a building, or even a shopping center. It may begin with one store and grow into an entire complex of stores, each appealing to a different trade, but by their very union growing together, until entire communities spring around them. At the finish of her speech her sagging jowls are redder than the cobblestones of my beloved town, redder than the scarlet jerseys worn by the hateful San Francisco 49ers. She stands majestic by my shredded curtains (done with my own teeth during an intergalaxy fight with Glutar), her button nose arched into the air of unlimited possibility.

"Yes" is what I tell her that day, every day. A hearty shake of my acne-coated face and a deep gut-reaction "Yes." "Yes" to Mother Freda as she sits in the corner of the garage, the light pouring through the dusty window to reveal masses of cobwebs tangled in her braided hair. From the lawn chair I watch paint flying from her crusty brushes, onto the hood of the Chevrolet, onto the ceiling, onto the chalky bags of lawn fertilizer, onto the garden trowels and broken rakes which line the paint-dashed walls. Paint everywhere from Mother Freda. Even streaming down the canvas and into the deep wrinkles of Mother Freda's thighs.

After three hours every Sunday she emerges from her "loft" looking like The Heap, a huge mound of greasy slime who is a hero of D.C. Comics. No matter how busy I am with my Town (and there is much to be done; unknown invaders attack our prosperous seaports, black plagues are rumored in the provinces), I do not miss the opportunity to stand by the screen door, clap whistle stomp my feet.

"Three cheers for Mother Freda," I yell, "she who is not fractured by the flotsam and jetsam of this painful ordeal."

My good-natured cheers earn me Mother's smile, a smile made earthly by the gap between her teeth.

"Look," she coos, holding up the still-dripping canvas.

Between the horizontal agonies of random smudges is a figure. Why Freda how marvelous, a blond maiden tripping over green blot (grass), a silver milk can dangling from one gnarled finger. Why Freda how divine. And in the upper corner there, yes it is indeed Mr. Sun, spreading his sopping warmth from the canvas to you.

"You like?" she asks, sounding like Dondi.

I gingerly move my hand from my chin and blow her a kiss. She stumbles across the gravel, her fat, paint-ooze arms as open as her mouth. Too late to dodge; I am pressed into the slippery, dripping bosom of this mighty beast my mother, Mother Freda.

V.
Collecting Payment

On that gray and rainy day, I am running into Pop Acorn's little neighborhood store. My father is in there with wispy-haired Pop. They are reading Nazi magazines. Though my father is an intelligent man, he cannot resist stories about atrocities. I hear them and begin to speak:

"Daddy . . . Daddy . . . something horrible has happened. Over at Govan's Little League field. That man, Ichman, who is supposed to be in America. Well, he was over there. Walking his dog. I know it was him, Daddy. I know from Scar. He said, 'Hey come here kid, me an' you is gonna have a house party.' Oh those eyes of his, Dad, those terrible eyes."

I pretend I am going to faint, and feel Pop Acorn's bony fingers grab my back. My father is in a rage.

"Eichmann at the ball park, hey? Not impossible. It's right

here in Scar that they suspect him to be in New York, and if he might be up there, then he could also be down here."

"Sure," says Pop Acorn, drooling. "Baltimore's the town all these Mafia guys come because the heat's on somewheres else. You'd better take a look."

While I take small gasps of air and make weird sighs, my father smashes his hand on a Wheaties box. He tells Pop that it might seem crazy, "but my son and I are gonna visit that ball park, and if we don't report back in two hours, call the fuzz." Pop nods gravely. Then he winks at me and makes a clucking sound. It is the only time I have ever heard him laugh.

Crouched behind the wheel, my father tugs at his soiled trench-coat collar. We ride in absolute silence. Every so often I give small neck jerks.

"I'll tell you one thing," he says finally. "Even if Eichmann gives me the slip today, I won't rest until I get the bastard. I'll haunt the ball park. You can believe that, son."

He is gnashing his teeth.

"That bastard even touches you or any of your little friends, I'll break his Nazi ass. Those queer boy Nazis are pretty effective against helpless kikes and little kids, but it'll be honky do re mi when I get my hands on him."

He is pounding the dashboard furiously, narrowly missing a coal truck, as we sweep in to the curb. Then we are leaping out of doors, into the mud. I stand close by his side, shivering and pointing to center field.

"There he is, Dad," I stutter. "He's out in the grass. It's *Ick-man*."

"I see him, son. Don't faint, I won't let you down."

My father slams me on the back and bounds around the rotting stands. In a flash he's across first base, streaking for

17

center field. Ten feet away, the startled doggy-walker turns and gives a little cry of terror.

"You've had it this time, Eichmann," screams my father.

I stand in the dark rain, watching the arms and legs tangle in the slick grass.

VI.
Life Among the Primates

Mr. Pensy, our eighth-grade teacher, has a huge ass. The huge ass is responsible for the fact that Mr. Pensy is still with us, for if he had a normal-size ass, he would have gone through the open window. Our class saw from the first day that Mr. Pensy is a mark. He told us that if we all did our very best, there would be nothing to worry about, but if we didn't, he wasn't going to fool around with us. We would just have "Nasty" written across the top of our report card and that would be that. We would also have a red "Nasty" written across our permanent record, and later on in life, when we went to get jobs, the red "Nasty" would stand out above all we had accomplished. We would be laughed out of the business world.

These remarks brought a unity to the class that had not before existed. I turned slowly and looked out of the corner of my eye at a Jew named Levin. He winked back. Other people did likewise. Mr. Pensy was going to be in for a rough time.

The second day of class, Mr. Pensy is trying to show us how an isosceles triangle works. He is hit in the head with an eraser. When he turns around, everyone is silent. Mr. Pensy decides to let the first offense go, and continues to tell us about A and B. He calls Levin to the front of the room and hands him a rubber-tipped pointer. Levin breaks the pointer over his knee, says "Here, Prick" and hands both halves back to Mr. Pensy. Mr. Pensy gets a girlish look of terror on his face and demands that Levin leave the room. Levin faints and is dragged into the hall by Grossman, who shouts that Pensy is a "Jew-hating murderer."

On the third day, Renus, a boy with one of the last of the ducktail haircuts who wears his Luckies rolled up in his sleeve, tells us that Mr. Pensy is a trolley-car driver in the summertime. When we enter class (twenty minutes late, at Levin's request) Mr. Pensy is greeted with a cattlelike roar of "Ding Dong Pensy." It is here that Mr. Pensy first tries to leap out of the window. We scream as his ass gets jammed and he is forced to come back inside.

During the semester, a boy in class becomes as badly thought of as Mr. Pensy. His name is Smart and he has a loud mouth, gray skin and wears rippled-sole shoes. Whenever Mr. Pensy needs someone to take the rap, we scream "Smart did it, sir," or "Mange did it. It was most definitely the Mange." Mr. Pensy invariably believes us, and keeps Mange after school. One month Mange is taken out of class and put into Baltimore Memorial Hospital. He has hepatitis and may die. For two days we all feel guilty but on the third day Mr. Pensy wants to know who shit on his chair (Renus did, after lunch) and we all scream "Mange." We go from the classroom happy

20

to have been liberated from regarding Mange as a human being.

Later on in the semester, Walter joins our class. He has been thrown out of an A-course section for piling up old sandwiches in the back of the room. Walter is very witty and says things under his breath, while erasers and pens books and slide rules sail up at Mr. Pensy. I never fail to break into helpless gales of laughter at Walter's remarks. Mr. Pensy catches us and keeps us after school. By the end of the day, his room is like a department store after a serious fire. Squashed apples, tomatoes and pears drip from the blackboard. Chocolate candy bars grease the legs of chairs. Pencils and sharp objects (many knives) sit in clusters on Mr. Pensy's desk, which features a crude carving with the caption MR. PENSY SUCKS A PENIS. Mr. Pensy looks up at us with exhausted, wrinkled eyes and asks us why we always talk in class. I stare at my book *The Wonderful World of Geometry*, and listen to Walter:

"We do not talk in class, sir. It's the Mange . . . I mean it's Smart."

"Smart?" says Mr. Pensy.

"That's right, sir," says Walter. "Smart has been reading a book called *How To Be a Ventriloquist* and throws his voice across the room. He has it in for Ward and I because we won't help him disrupt the class."

"That's right, a ventriloquist," I say.

"A ventriloquist," says Mr. Pensy.

Mr. Pensy picks up one of the confiscated fountain pens and writes "Smart is a ventriloquist." He sits there rubbing his square head for a few seconds, then demands that we come to the office with him.

At the office Mr. Pensy dials the phone with thick certain gestures. He stares between us, his eyes burning with rage.

21

"Hello, Mrs. Smart, this is Pensy at City High. Your son is a ventriloquist."

From the look of horror on Mr. Pensy's face we know that Mrs. Smart has told him that the Mange is back in the hospital with a relapse of hepatitis. We watch as Mr. Pensy drops the phone and attempts to leap through the office window. He does not fit and becomes wedged in, his bulging ass shaking to and fro like a giant Jell-O.

During the last few weeks of the semester, Mr. Pensy decides to give us a test every day. He stands slumped in the front of the classroom, his brown double-breasted suit buttoned in the wrong holes, his red blotched face squelched in a leer.

"Every test will count. If you don't know the work, it's your tough luck." He hands out small yellow sheets of paper and puts an impossible problem on the board. While he is drawing it, we are all writing things like "Eat a Wet One, Pensy" in big black letters. Thomas Gurn, a friend of Renus, who wears silk jackets with pictures of Mount Fujiyama on the back, takes the papers up to him. Gurn's penis is protruding from his pleated pants.

"Here Mr. Penthy thir. Here are the testies. Even dumb pricks [points to his fly] like us know the answers to thuth easy quethtions."

Mr. Pensy's hands shake uncontrollably and he runs for the window. This time the seat of his pants burst and we are treated to a giant birthmark on his hairy ass. He still does not fit through.

VII.
Art and Celery

Up in the attic, among the cobwebs and spiders and half-shapes, I find an old trunk with my father's artwork in it.

"Wow, Warren," I say. "My father used to be an artist."

"Undoubtedly a Norman Rockwell . . ."

"No. Look at these."

Wiping off the dust, I pull out a portfolio filled with great cartoons. Cartoons of the Kaiser, cartoons of Baron von Richthofen, wearing an eyepatch. Underneath the baron is the caption A REAL MAN. Next to him is a cartoon of a deacon, long face and hanging jowls. Caption: THE FALSE FACE OF HUMILITY.

"Warren," I say, "do you know what we have found?"

"What?"

"My old man's Town of Thatched Rooves."

Excitedly, I whip through a box of ancient dresses, old baby shoes, Gene Autry wristwatches (two of them; one of them was broken when I bashed Walter in the head), broken Mix-masters and a moldy Hoover vacuum cleaner. Then I hit the jackpot. A roll of green tagboard, wrapped with a blue rubber band. I slide the band off and the picture springs to life. It's wonderful. A huge landscape of dinosaurs, winged leather birds and great hairy mammoths with gigantic ivory tusks. All of them sitting in charcoal slime, while up above lightning flashes, and one strange fish stares at the sun.

"Incredible. Who would have thought old Glenn?"

"Come on," says Warren. "He probably copied it out of a National Geographic."

"So what? Even if he did, that fish in the corner is some-thing he added himself. I know it is. It's got style."

Suddenly a great change comes over me. I want to race downstairs, grab my old man. I want to tell him that his Town of Thatched Rooves is alive and well, that it no longer has to hold its breath. I want to show him that his prehistoric mon-sters are breathing, finished with gagging in the dank attic.

I race down the steps and leap into the living room. Mother Freda is sitting next to the window. She is reading a book by Aleister Crowley called *Magick, in Theory and Practice*. This week she is "researching the black magicians" for her Garden Club lecture.

"Bobby," she says, "you should stay. I find these old books so stimulating."

"You're lying," I say. "I checked the book mark. You haven't been reading it at all. You just stare at it."

Instantly her facade crumbles. I don't know why I attacked her. She shakes her head and begins to cry.

"Oh God, God," she says. "I wish I were a magician. God how I'd love to disappear. But it's no use crying. I've no one to blame but myself. I could have married Ronald Hogan. He would have understood my sensitive side."

"Speaking of that," I say, spreading the drawings open on the floor, "just what do you make of these? Aren't they terrific?"

She looks at the cartoons and then the monsters. She bites her lower lip.

"Oh, those old things," she sighs. She waves her arm like Marie Antoinette.

"What do you mean?" I scream. I can't believe my ears. Here is living proof that Glenn existed outside of *Scar* magazine and oozing cysts.

"Do not scream at me," she whines. "It'll give me the pins and needles."

Pins and needles. That's her new thing. Last week it was spastic fingers, and the week before that trick elbows. (She would lay her fat arms on the kitchen table and her "bad nerves" would cause her elbows to fly up. It made her look like Red Skelton doing his sea gull routine.)

"I would never want to give you the pins and needles," I say, "and I know that you could have married the missionary. But how can you dismiss these? Glenn drew them. I mean, they are damn good."

Before she can answer, my old man walks through the door. Dramatic entrances are a habit of his. I am certain he waits until the most opportune moment to attack, and I feel a surge of admiration for his new style.

He is carrying a shopping bag, and some celery is sticking above his forehead. I suddenly picture him as some great, blossoming vegetable. He will lie down and Mother Freda will grate him up, cover him with her blue cheese.

"Dad," I say, "I found the Town . . . I mean the cartoons. They are great, really."

"Celery," my old man says. "This goddamned celery. It tried to leap out of the bag all the way home. And if I pressed

25

it to my face to keep the son of a bitch in the bag, then it tickled me. They get you any way you look, Freda. You turn left—whammmm. You turn right—mash. Any way at all. What's this?"

He has finally noticed the cartoons spread out in front of him.

"Great," I say. "Would you show me how to draw?"

"The last person I showed how to paint was her," he says. He points at Freda. Instantly she is upon him.

"That's it," she says, "call me 'her.' I don't mind. It's quite all right. Old 'her' will do the dishes. Old 'her' will sit up all night when you have the measles. I don't mind. Really. Here, you want to come over here and laugh at me. Why don't you? Old 'her' wouldn't mind."

"Fucking celery," says my old man. It's drooping out of the bag and he is propping it with his chin. Finally, he drops the entire bag of groceries on the rug.

Freda screams. "That's it. God, that's just what old 'her' wants. You dumb bastard."

She is hopping off her chair, bounding around my father, who is laughing and waving the celery in her eyes.

"See how it tickles," he yells. "See?"

Her blue chemise is swirling in the air. Her ringlets are springing off her head and she is flailing her arms at my father like a flabby windmill. He tickles her face, again and again. She lunges after him now, and he leaps back and steps on the Kaiser. They are locked in battle above me and I am trying to gather up the dinosaurs but it's too late. Her high heels catch the fish on the sun and rip open his intestines. The red rug shows through. I know it's his blood.

"You bastard," she screams as they whirl around the room. "Gimme that celery now. Gimme it."

I grab the drawings again, but Freda's heel catches the

corner of a paper and rips it to shreds. She reaches down and pulls them out of my hand, puts them in her mouth and chews wildly. My old man picks up the Dinty Moore Beef Stew and hurls it at her. And I am screaming then, Wait a minute, wait, save the cartoons, don't eat them, Freda, don't eat the Town, wait, wait, will you just wait a goddamned minute and stop stop stop stop stop. I mean don't, no. Will you look at those cartoons?

VIII.
The Hangy Wangy

Bent beneath neon. I am with Kirk and Walter. We have taken to hanging out at the shopping center. We watch each other's acne, twice as red and lumpy inside this purple glare. With us is fat Baba Looie. Later on he will choke to death on a submarine sandwich, and most people will be delighted. But now he is our hero. Among the three of us, Kirk is Baba's personal favorite. Walter is feared and disliked because he looks like a baby professor. I am too nervous. Only Kirk has won the fat heart of Baba.

Now Baba slouches in front of Read's Drug Store, his big hands running through his greasy scalp, his cigarette drooping to his button-down shirt. His stomach rolls over his s-t-r-e-t-c-h belt and his chinos are a crumpled mass (crumpled from battles, I am certain. I get hard-ons dreaming of battles, Baba beside me, chains in Polack faces, myself in shining shopping cart, Baba wheeling me through downtown Baltimore, both of

28

us carrying underground bombs, dealing death and destruction to everything in our path. Some nights I dream of Baba and myself killing Kirk, dragging him through dark places, his organs spread over the macadam like a run-over dog's. Great guilt comes over me for this dream, and I spend days being Kirk's devoted friend to make up for it).

We are waiting for Baba to do the Hangy Wangy. It is an event and Kirk, by laughing with Baba and cutting a riff about where we should put old people, has convinced him that we are worthy of witnessing Baba's art. (And a good riff it was too. Listen to Kirk's voice filling up the great hole that is Baba's ego: "I'll tell you one thing, Baba. Man, we got to get rid of them old people. We got to *do* 'em. And I got just the plan. We take all the old people and throw them in the Grand Canyon. That's right, just throw them in there. Get a bunch of young cats with whips and things. Move it along, old people. Keep it going. Just pushing whole long lines of 'em in the Grand Canyon. You dig it? Then, when we got 'em all in there, we get you to come over 'em in a Sopwith Camel, and bomb 'em with grandfather's clocks, old butter churns, wine-stained piano stools, stuff you copped from their houses. [Baba loves that. He begins his slow lizard smile and deep throaty laugh. We all join him.] So, dig, once we weight those old mothers down with all that stuff, you can shoot gas in on 'em. That's right, gas. Just shoot it right in and that's the end of those old cocksuckers, pronto. . . .") Baba is nearly falling off his shoppers' bench over this, and the rest of us lean back with him. When he puts his arm around Kirk, I feel great pangs of jealousy.

But such small emotions die quickly in the grandeur of the Hangy Wangy. Baba stands below the aluminum roof, waiting for the last group of shoppers to go to their cars. Then, with one mighty effort, he hawks mouth saliva onto the ceiling.

29

It is a great dripping loogie, one that looks very much like a Chesapeake Bay oyster. We watch it hanging there, slowly starting to come down, and then like a Duncan Yo-Yo walking the dog, it springs back to its base. Kirk is beside himself with glee. Walter and I lean confidently, content to be second lieutenants in Baba's army. Down and up, down and up . . . An old man with a veiny nose and ragamuffin coat comes under it but escapes. Two businessmen, fitting recipients, leer at us but fate has dealt the hanger to someone else.

Finally it happens. A mother comes out of Read's with her small son. They stand (oh great joy) beneath the swaying spittle, the child eagerly holding out his hand to receive his model Kitty Hawk. Splatttt—the full force of the spittle lands on their outstretched arms. We scream. We howl (keeping one eye on Baba; will he notice us, will he fully appreciate our loyalty?). Kirk is slamming himself against the drugstore windows. Walter is hammering a trash can. I am rolling on the warm cement, laughing, crying. The woman is screaming at us, trying desperately to find a handkerchief. The spittle has taken on a life of its own, growing down both their arms. It's too much. It's beautiful. The Hangy Wangy.

IX.
Heart to Heart

Walter and I go to the pipe. I sit on top of the pipe and hang my legs over. Walter slides down the muddy bank and flips rocks into the stream.

"What did you get out of the Hangy Wangy?" I ask.

"A few giggles."

I hate answers like that. Typical of girls who will later become telephone operators.

He is shaking his pear-shaped head and rubbing his stomach. The sun is glinting off the steel rims of his glasses.

"You know, Walter," I say, "you always rub your stomach when you're lying."

"Huh? What do you mean?"

"Your stomach . . . You rub your stomach."

"So? I rub my stomach. Lying about what, smart ass?"

It's not like Walter to say "giggles" or "smart ass." He is quiet and poetic, but lately we have both been influenced by

31

the language of Baba and the gang. On some days I feel myself turn fat and soft. Feel my legs get short and dumpy. Then I know that Baba has taken over my speech, my style, all of me. It's a transformation just as great as when we pretended we were cowboys on the hill. Greater. For this transformation is involuntary, and brings with it guilt and fear.

"Let's be honest," I say. "I got sick after what we did at the shopping center. At the time it was funny. But . . . it wasn't really, you know?"

I am trembling as I speak. It is no good for a delinquent to have a conscience. I will not drink water, and Warren will become so dry he cannot speak to me from my chest.

"It *was* funny," he says, not looking at me. "I thought it was then, and I still do. The way that lady looked. Don't be sorry about it. She would have done the same to you. Like Glenn and Freda. You know that. They want one thing. To turn you into them. Little replicas. Don't be soft."

I am overwhelmed. I want to fall in the dirt in front of Walter and beg forgiveness for my candy assness. I want to run into a Golden Age Club and knock around domino players. I will strangle my own grandfather. Hot flushes are all over me. I have to stick with my friends. We are rebels. We are a brutish, unstoppable force.

"Yeah," I say to Walter. "Yeah, yeah."

"In fact," says Walter, lighting a cigarette and popping a Benzedrine pill, "I think it was so funny that I'm going back down the shopping center tonight to see it again."

"Well, screw you," I say.

Oh my God. Why did I say that? I grab my chin, shut my lying mouth.

But now something strange happens. Walter is rubbing his stomach furiously. And he is saying to himself over and over,

"Yeah, jes go right down there and see it again and again. Every night. Gonna do those old people in."

And I feel lightheaded. Walter is Kirk and Baba. I am Kirk and Baba. Glenn is Freda. I am Kirk and Baba and Freda. The sun is in the sky. The sewer water rushes from the pipe, foul, brown and clogged with old tires, candy wrappers and rubbers. And I sit still, sit very still, listening to the incessant, terrified beating of a heart. But whose heart? Whose?

X.
The End of Innocence and All That

I am downtown in Hutzule's Department Store with Kirk and Randy. We are into our heavy shoplifting phase. For the occasion we wear inconspicuous sweaters with school letters ironed on the pockets. Shoplifting is full of ritual and deep emotions. You begin by sticking a magazine inside your shirt. My choice is *Pro Football Highlights*, which features many action shots of Johnny Unitas. Just lately, Johnny Unitas has started giving me cold sweats and erections. After copping the magazine, we glide into the Record Nook. On the walls of this department are pennants from all the high schools in the area, and black cardboard musical notes, which look as if they could leap to the floor and entertain you. After looking out of the corner of our eyes, we pick 45s off short, round racks (reminiscent of Baba Looie's cock, so delightful in the shower after gym class). We carry the records into listening booths and put them inside the stolen magazine. I place mine

34

next to a picture of Johnny Unitas warding off monstrous Negro linemen and imagine juices secreting from each groove.

Then *it* happens. Randy sees *it* first and reports his wisdom to me with great relish. His small eyes (set like frozen peas in a round of red pork) glisten and dance. His chubby chin trembles and jumps as if pulled by wire. He is ecstatic to have scored a first because he lives entirely through me. On many days he will mindlessly repeat every witticism I utter. Often I will set a designated number in my mind and when Randy repeats that number of my sayings I will give him the Fingee. It is a cruel and barbarous torture, the Fingee, and makes maximum use of Randy's gullibility. I ask him for his fist, promising not to squeeze it hard. Then I press the bent, pink fingers into his palm, which sends massive waves of pain up Randy's portly arm into his always surprised face. Randy submits to this indignity because Kirk, Walter and I constantly tell him I am a genius.

But today, I must admit, Randy has turned a trick. He tells me in his best Arkansas Ecstatic voice:

"I seen yo' daddy over in the corner wif his arm round some ole girl."

"Thank you thank you, Randy," I say, placing my hand over his sweating fist. After Randy turns red, I tell Kirk.

"Traumatic," says Kirk, completely detached. He is much too busy trying to make time with the salesgirl, who wears lace dickeys and possesses a gigantic pair of tits.

Hiding behind Ladies' Lingerie, Randy and I observe my father. He is indeed with another woman. She is Delores Conklin, secretary of the Waverly Methodist Church. My father is affecting a sporty look. He is wearing a black cardigan with red trim and silver buttons. On his long head is a plaid racing cap which is set at a jaunty angle. From his mouth hangs a pipe. He thinks he is Perry Como. His right arm is tossed casually over Delores' broad back. I am terribly disappointed with his style. Delores looks like a Polish ham smothered in some gooey brown sauce. Or like Mother Freda.

After waving good-bye to Kirk, who has managed to get himself behind the record rack and is fondling Miss Tits, Randy and I follow my father to the street. He stops next to Delores and hails a cab. He is a nervous wreck.

Because of heavy traffic, we are able to follow the lovers on foot. The cab turns up Cathedral Street and pulls to a stop at the Hotel Albion. Delores springs from her seat. I now notice a dying yellow flower sagging from the lapel of her pea green suit. As they hurry into the lobby, she leaves a petal trail.

"Whad we gonna do?" says Randy.

"Teach my father the virtues of faithfulness and the responsibilities of fatherhood," I reply.

"Whad?" says Randy.

"Get your money ready, Randy."

After a suitable waiting period, we enter the lobby. It is exactly as I would have pictured it. Wonderful old men staring into the past beside rotted palms, forlorn reception desk from 1936 motion picture. The room clerk is another cliché. He pretends ignorance of the matter, suggesting a tip from my father. I use my basso buffo voice and tell him that my uncle is Judge Surrento from criminal court, which is true. I show him a press clipping (which I have with me at all times, even now) of the judge handing down long sentences to members of a Baltimore crime wave. This impressive fact enables us to obtain the room number and a personal escort to the freight elevator. Before we enter the elevator, Randy hands the man five dollars.

"Why did you give the man five dollars?" I ask, as we move through the gloom.

"Ya sade git ma money ready," says Randy.

I patiently explain to Randy that the money was to be given only in the event that the clerk did not fall for the bluff. I apply a wicked Fingee. Randy screams.

Once on the fourth floor, I get a drink of water from an ancient fountain. Randy asks me, "Whad ya gonna do?"

"Patience, Randy."

I wait for a full ten minutes, sitting on the dusty hallway runner, reading about Johnny Unitas and how he can win games in the last two minutes. True to form, I break out in the cold sweats and feel the beginnings of an erection. At the end of a paragraph full of players' testimonials concerning Johnny Unitas' ice-water veins, I rise. I ask Randy to slap me in the face. He mutters that he cannot do it because I am his friend and a genius. I demand it. Randy looks down at his feet, which point in opposite directions. He still cannot do it. I take his hand and squeeze until his face turns red and past red to white. He grits his small teeth and slaps my face with great violence. Tears spring from my eyes. Chills tear my body. After hiding Randy in the stairwell, I rap madly at room 45.

"Daddy, Daddy," I say in a voice suggesting controlled panic. "What are you doing in there?"

"Oh God," whispers my father from the other side of the wall.

"Daddy, Daddy," I say, much louder now and high-pitched like a bird screaming over the death of her young.

"Jesus God, Glenn," says Delores Conklin.

"Daddddddddddddeeeeeeeeeee," I yell with blood-curdling accuracy.

"Daddddddddddddeeeeeeeeeee, how could you? Mother was such a nice girl. She coulda married the missionary."

Now I am kicking the door, scraping at the transom, throwing myself all over the hall.

"Dadddddddddddeeeeeeeeeeeeeeeeeeeeeeeeeeeeee."

I jiggle the bronze doorknob, burst into the lovers' room. Delores Conklin's bra is hanging off her shoulders. My father is making futile efforts to put on his pants. Both of them are chanting that there are some things a boy just can't understand. I roll around on the rug for a while, gasping wheezing moaning. *Oh*, I say to myself, *this is joy, this must be joy.*

XI.
Clothesline

It seems impossible, but it has happened. The Colts have lost. The setting was perfect for Johnny Unitas. Two minutes to play, the Redskins ahead fourteen to ten, the Colts with the ball on their own forty yard line. A perfect pass from Johnny Unitas to Raymond Berry, who makes an amazing tightwire snare at the sideline, two disgusting Redskin backs hanging on his shoulders, puts us on their twenty. Kirk gives a knowing nod, and I leap up, the cold sweats pouring over my body ten times worse than a junkie's cold turkey. First fucking down, with one minute thirty-two seconds showing on the scoreboard clock. During time out, I walk through the knotty pine section of Kirk's basement to the dingy storage room and put my head in the freezer. The sweat dries on my body as I take deep, deep breaths.

Action resumes. No gain on a line plunge. I am scraping my face and making small noises from my stomach. It's clear

39

what my beloved Johnny U. is up to. Keeping them honest for the slant-in pass. I see it before it happens. Down and out, and then in, like a gazelle. The ball will float over the grubby hands of Redskin linemen, sail through the maze of terrified Redskin defenders, into the waiting arms of whoever Johnny has decided will gain the moment of absolute glory.

I feel the erection pressing my black Levi's to the bursting point. The Colts are up in formation. I hear Johnny's voice bark the signals, the cool stiletto syllables fracturing the despicable spirits of those thirty thousand Redskin rooters. He is back in the pocket. He is setting up. My pants are on fire, I tell you. Oh God, he is crushed. Smothered by a mammoth wall of Redskin fat. The dust clears. The cruel linemen stalk back to their side. Jesus fucking Christ, he doesn't move. He lies still, frozen in time. Not moving. There is a flurry of activity, a stretcher. The word itself is enough to make me bite my wrist, which I do until blood comes from small holes.

"They can't," I say, tears drowning me.

"Dig Ward," says Kirk.

"Ha Ha Ha," says Walter.

My friends circle around me. Their faces are distorted into blowfish. I am beside myself with grief. I stand quivering from the bottom lip, aware that I am the laughingstock, but too horrified to care.

"Agh, agh" is all I am able to muster. The distorted faces dance around me, pointing and shouting. From far away, as if from a tunnel, I hear grim Chuck Thompson announcing the worst.

"And the final score is Washington Redskins fourteen, Baltimore Colts ten."

His metal voice goes on to relate the Unitas injury.

"It is impossible to say how bad John was shaken up on the

40

play. We can only pray that he has the wind knocked out of him."

Kirk is in focus now. He is pretending to fade back for a pass. Walter is lumbering after him, his arms raised above his bleating face. Kirk is mocking Johnny U. by making whimpering cries of terror.

"No pleathe Mr. Redskin do not harm me."

I cannot stand it. I feel a bomb, old and rusty, explode in my head.

"You rotten inhuman bastards," I yell, feeling like a complete fool.

They are deaf to my pleas, and continue their obscene play, Kirk getting more frantic in his defense. He falls to his knees and begs Walter not to hurt him, swears he will call Walter's mother if he "lays one silly hand on him." I feel myself storm across the room, leave my feet at high velocity. My body parallel to the ground, like Jim Thorpe's flying wedge, my arms out like Don Schinnick as he clotheslines a Green Bay Packer. I crash into them, smash them into the television. Kirk's arm slams through the screen. Walter cracks his head on a picture of Kirk's brother, Chuckie, a grim Marine. I stand above them and feel like Superman or Johnny Unitas after a four-touchdown afternoon. The blood is racing through my body. My chest is growing inches of solid muscle.

"That's for Johnny U. and the Baltimore Colts," I say. Then I turn and begin my long walk down the ramp, away from the defeated jackals. I am Weeb Ewbank after the 1958 championship game.

Unlike Weeb, I do not make it. Something clips me from behind. There is a forearm smash to my nose and a huge pileup in the center of the room. I am scrambling for my life, looking for an opening, as cleats stomp my face. Where the

41

hell is the referee? Fifteen yards here for sure. I manage to gain my balance and stiff-arm Kirk as he swoops in for the kill. I am streaking for daylight; the stands go wild. Then the lights go out, deflated footballs spin through gray smoke, all of the Town of Thatched Rooves watches my burial out beyond the flaming grandstand.

When I come to, I see a tree limb in front of a yellow light. Am I on the training table? No, it's the moon. I try to rise but every muscle has been ripped, every tendon torn. It will be weeks before I am able to move. Where am I? What's up?

The stars are out above me, cold winds push across my bleeding legs. I think that I am in a little park not far from my home. It seems important to stay awake, and I pull out a couple of blades of grass and tickle my eyeballs. I figure that if I irritate myself enough, I will not fall into a frozen coma.

After I fall asleep, I dream of myself in a long white room, a hospital ward, I suppose. On the walls are films of the Baltimore Colts. Five movies running simultaneously, with the sound tracks overlapping one another, until all that can be made out is one high-pitched scream. Next to me, propped up in traction, is Johnny U. He lies very still, staring blankly at the movies. Nurses walk by, dressed as cheerleaders, occasionally stopping to spread their white legs for Johnny. He smiles and says "Down set." They begin to take off their clothes and fall upon him, but he stops them and points to me.

"I'm crackers over the Bobby boy. Make love to him and I'll watch."

"Thank you, wonderful Johnny U.," I say, as the movies flash on and on. . . .

My dream is interrupted by Kirk and Walter, who offer me their hands. I tell them that it is simply half time and I am

42

just taking a breather. They merge into one face, tell me that they had no choice but to clothesline me. I see the cheerleaders behind them. Johnny U. passing a ball from the tops of trees. The wind is sweeping over me, old programs from 1948 Colt games piling up beside my eyes. I come awake for an instant as they drop me, like old, scarred equipment, into the back seat of Kirk's car.

XII.
In Which Somebody Misses the Point

I walk into the living room with my box of records. It's a red plastic box with a gold snap and inside it are jewels gold rarest pearls. Ah, those 45s: Specialty labels—black and yellow with Little Richard screaming "Tutti Frutti" or "I Hear You Knockin'"; Sun labels—yellow and brown with Carl Perkins doing "Blue Suede Shoes" and "Honey, Don't"; ABC Paramount labels—black with a twisting red snake across the letters, and Danny and the Juniors doing "Rock 'n' Roll Is Here to Stay" and "At the Hop"; RCA—the label is austere but they have Elvis Presley and I remember the first time I heard "Heartbreak Hotel." Even though it was just a year or so ago it is already a moment with instant nostalgia, infinite wonder. I was sitting down the basement listening to the "Buddy Bean Show" and they were playing a lot of bad stuff (Kay Starr doing "Rock and Roll Waltz"), and then Buddy said, "Yes, that was Kay Starr, but now I've got something a little different for you, something that could make a mighty big splash in Hitsville, and here it is, a newcomer to the scene, folks, but one we here at WZX think just might be around a long time." And then they put it on. Strange is the only word I can think of to describe it. Strange, and desolate and lonely, and that was fine with me, because I was feeling that way myself, lost in my fantasy world again. That song opened it all up to me. Not only Elvis but all the records I had, and have collected since, seem to take on gigantic powers, secret misty visions, or brash cartoon miracles, and they flash on-off in my head every time I play them—pictures and whispers, and groans, a weird magic which never fails no matter how many times I play them. These are more than records. These are the Real World.

So I sit down in front of my pink square plastic 45 automatic magic maker and put on a stack. The putting on of records is a ritual that is so deep with hidden significance that I break out in a sweat every second. Tonight I want to compare Gene Vincent with Elvis and Carl Perkins. So I put "Be-Bop-A-Lula" on and then "Boppin' the Blues" (Perkins) and finally "I Got a Woman" by Elvis. I will listen to all of them, make faces when the gritty guitars really start to wind up; I'll feel strong and deep and real. Yes, and maybe I'll add another Sun record, Warren Brown's "Ubangi Stomp." It's new, and it's a typical Sun special. For every company has its own mystique, much greater than the mere sound. With Sun records you picture hot dusty towns, and maybe Carl Perkins' girl friend is out in that town, doing it up without him, and you can see it all, every bit of it. Or maybe Warren Brown is actually in the jungle and he is stomping his feet, and the Captain is there next to him, and you are there too, without a doubt, without a care in the world. Yes, next to my Town there is only one thing of any significance—my records. For after this night of listening to them I will lie in bed and the Town of Thatched Rooves will be even more substantial. I will see everything with a crystal clearness. Music makes all the buildings stand out. Sun City and my Town are one in that moment, and there can be no threats from Fernando Roush, none at all.

"Yes, you will really have some visions tonight," says Warren.

And I will, pure beauty. Nothing can stop me.

"Will you turn that thing off?" says Glenn.

"What?"

"I'm trying to read."

"I'll turn it down."

"Listen, I want it off. That stuff is horrible. Sounds like a bunch of niggers."

My anger is limitless. I want to race across the room and make an all-out attack on him.

I decide to ignore him and put on "The Book of Love," by the Monotones. When you hear that song, you actually see a huge black book with a golden binding, and perhaps you will step into that book and inside it will be a city with spires, and sandstone towers, and you know that city is yours, all yours, your own Town of Thatched Rooves.

"Listen, turn it off. Anyway, I want to tell you about this book I'm reading."

"I don't want to hear about your book. I don't care about your goddamn Nazis."

I expect to get a rise out of him with that, but tonight he is playing the patient father. How I hate him.

"No, this isn't Nazis. It's different. Something you'd like. Let me tell you about it."

The son of a bitch. He has just taken you out of the hop. Danny and the Juniors are there, and there are big orange streamers on the wall, and this blond-haired teen-age sex queen is twisting in front of you, and your old man wants to tell you about another one of his Nazi books.

"The name of this book is *Man's Fate*," says my father. "It's by a Frenchman. . . ."

A Frenchman. What do they know about rock 'n' roll? Once every six months some French singer comes on TV and does bush league versions of Little Richard. Worse than Pat Boone.

But I try to listen. I really do. If he gets the story over with, it'll be time for him to go into the bathroom.

"See, this takes place in China . . ."

"I thought you said a Frenchman wrote it."

"It's a novel. They can take place anywhere. It's about a revolution. There are these guys called the Kumattang . . ."

As his voice drones on, as he slips and shuffles over the Chinese names (which all sound alike), I sit and finger my records, and images of the Big Bopper, and Buddy Holly, and Ritchie Valens, three rock 'n' roll singers who got killed in a plane crash, come into mind. I see the plane going down and Buddy Holly singing "That'll Be the Day" as the nose of that doomed craft buries itself in the earth. This image fills me with a great tenderness and longing.

"There will never be another Buddy Holly," I say.

"What?"

"Nothing. Go ahead."

And he does, but I am not with him at all. I am at a big party with Frankie Lymon and the Teen-Agers, and Fats Domino, and we are drinking red wine, all of us in the best pub in the Town of Thatched Rooves.

"So how do you like it?"

"Great, Dad. That's a hell of a story."

"Yeah . . . Well, it's getting late. I'll tell you the rest of it tomorrow. It's an important book."

"Sure," I say.

I watch him get up slowly, like a robot. When he walks into the other room, I shake my head.

"My poor old man," I say. "He's really missed the whole thing. My poor old man."

XIII.
In Which I Join the Aces

I do not want to be lurking on these cold apartment house steps. Walter does not want to be here either. You can tell because he isn't being poetic, isn't looking studious, isn't Walter. He's been terrified out of his name. As have I.

But we are here just the same. Here in the darkness waiting for the night watchman. It is our duty to cop his night watch, a beautiful gold number which hangs by a delicate chain from his gray pants loop. If we can bring this off, we will be invited to join Baba Looie's Five Aces, the toughest gang in this dull city. Only a few minutes ago, Baba dropped us off in the snow and gave us our orders. Kirk was with him, our friend Kirk, who has already been initiated into the Aces. He had to mug a grandmother in Sparrows Point Industrial Park and steal her sweater, an easy task, but then Baba has always been partial to Kirk. That's life, as Walter says in his more poetic moments.

I have wanted to be a member of a gang for years. I remember the first time I felt the desire sweep my body. I was reading Father's Man magazine, an article about some blind Greek kid who had been stabbed to death on the East Side. At first, I felt great spasms of remorse, but gradually, after seventeen rereadings, I came to understand that what really attracted me to the tale was the pictures of the gang. Tough, beautiful faces, faces with a kind of character, as Freda would say. I cut each of them out, Jim Prevus, Arthur Sphekus, Gus Cocoros, and pasted them to my wall. Afterward I placed a big tube of Testors glue under my nose and fell into a coma.

Tonight is my chance. I could feel my balls tighten as Baba appeared in front of Read's, his heavy body completely cloaked in black. From his right hand fell a blacker cane, with a silver wolf's-head knob. I could see myself walking with him down some dark hallway into the Aces' Lair. I could hear the Aces' voices low and cool, as they talked beneath the midnight-blue drapes, beneath the chains hanging so religious from the wall. I could see these same Aces under the hard light at the police station, not one sound coming from their lips. The police would be ruthless, trying every routine at their command. Fat cop, thin cop, nice cop, mean cop, but there would be nothing for any of them from my Aces, for no Ace would ever break the secret codes of the underworld. Yes, yes. I see a whole procession of cops throw up their arms in futility. I see the Ace's hand reach slowly to his black boot, to take a mighty pill from the sliding heel. A move so deft that only another Ace could possibly notice. Those wonderful Aces. I hear them chuckling softly at the mere idea of ever going straight.

So now I wait here with Walter, timid Walter, this silver gun in my hand.

"How in the world are we gonna ever pull this off?"

Walter again. He'll be a bad risk if trouble arises, but we have to do it together.

"It'll be easy," I say. "I come up . . . no, you come up and ask him for a match."

"Sure, and have the bastard identify me. You're outa your fucking mind."

I am tempted to remind Walter that I am packing the gun. I picture him dying in slow motion, myself running through the dark night full of joy and terror.

"Cool it," I tell him. "What kind of sock you got on?"

"You know I wear knee hose. They offer support."

"Take one of 'em off."

"You're gonna strangle me. Is it because of what happened to you after the Colt game? I didn't do anything. It was mainly Kirk."

I assure Walter that I have no intention of strangling him.

"Just take off the sock. He'll be here in five minutes. Hurry."

Walter sits on a frozen block of snow and unties his Scotch Grains. I balance the small gun in my hand. Light. Nifty. Probably made by some Ace craftsman in his leisure hours. It feels like a magic wand. But it also terrifies me. I picture the bullets falling into a puddle of snow. I picture the gun opening and me not being able to get it back together. This will not do for an Ace.

"My sock is off," says Walter.

I tell him the obvious. He'll put it over his head to eliminate the identity problem.

He tries, but it will not go over his head. He begins to whine. I am dying to whip him with my pistol. Here it is eleven twenty-seven, two minutes away from the action, and Walter's sock barely covers his forehead.

"What the hell am I going to do?" he cries.

"You are going to get that son of a bitch over your head. Pull."

"I can't, Ward. It just won't go." He is standing next to me now, his head snapped to his spine. The sock comes over one eye.

"Pull, Walter. Pull."

He pulls, grits his teeth. The sock finally comes down over both eyes. It occurs to me that I have made a crucial miscalculation. It will be extremely difficult for him to ask the night watchman for a match with any reasonable degree of spontaneity. I bite my wrist and begin to cry.

"Ward, Ward, where are you? I can't see a thing with this sock over my head."

I blow my nose between my fingers and dig at my cheeks.

"Ward, Ward, how the hell can I ask for a match?"

Walter is staggering around on the lawn, missing the evergreen by inches. As he falls into the snow I am inspired.

"That's it, Walter. Stay that way. Stagger around. It'll get his attention, and I can sneak up on him with the gun."

I hear footsteps approaching us and leap into a snow-covered bush.

"Hey there, young fella, what's the problem?"

"I . . . ah . . . got this sock on my head."

The man walks across the pavement to help Walter. I see the gold chain burrowing into his pocket. I imagine the watch turning green next to his dying skin. He is reaching down to the top of Walter's head. Walter is scrambling away from him on his knees, making small exclamation points of terror.

"Now come here, son. I'm not going to hurt you. You got it all wrong. You gotta help . . ."

"Get away from me," screams Walter.

"Let me help you with that sock, sonny. Somebody played a joke on you."

"Fuck off; leggo."

The old man is pulling the toe of the sock. Walter is on his knees, both hands clinging to the elastic. The old man is gain-

52

ing ground fast. Walter is exhausted. I step from the shadows.

"Cool it, old-timer, and hand over the night watch."

"What?"

The old man lets go of the sock and starts to turn. I try to belt him with the gun but he ducks and I hit Walter. Walter spins around and runs into the evergreen. The old man kicks me squarely in the nuts, and pulls out a barlow knife. I am doubled over in pain. Walter spins off the evergreen and butts into the old man's back. The old man is thrown forward and I clip him with the gun. He does not fall, but roars after me, slashing the knife wildly.

Walter is yelling, "Ward, the sock." The old man is yelling, "punk kids never git this night watch." I am dodging like mad as the old bastard hops after me, slashing red berries with his blade. Then I grab a high branch and swing in on him, kick him in the jaw, like Errol Flynn. He falls back into Walter, who screams "*My mmm-outh.*" Apparently Walter has been stabbed in the lip. I smack the old man in the head, punch his runny nose. He drops his knife, falls with a thud. Walter is still screaming "*My mmm-outh.*" Lights are going on all over this development. This is serious. I grab the old man's weapon, start to cut through his pants loop, when he clamps his mouth on my arm. I smash him good again. When I pull away, his false teeth hang from my wrist. Quickly I slice through the old material, reach into his pocket and grab the watch. I turn it over in my hand and read *To Zeke for fifty years valiant service.* Walter is still running around the tree fighting the sock and crying about his mouth. More lights. Lights everywhere. I grab Walter's hand and drag him back through the garages. We finally get the sock off and run as fast as possible to Kirk's. We have the watch. We're in the gang.

XIV.
The Bumjar

Though Walter and Kirk think I am crazy, the fact still remains—I am in love. It's really hopeless. I never figured for a moment that after joining the Five Aces, and taking drugs, I could fall for a girl like Susan. But I have—oh yes, I'm deep down the blue drain of love.

Susan is in my high school junior class and is wonderful in every aspect. Her breasts are well-rounded and she never wears black V-neck sweaters without a dickey underneath. Her hair is ratted to her head, but not so tight that it isn't springy and full of life. Her dresses come below her knee, and one of her penny loafers has a nickel in it. I sit in history class and think how clever it is of her to put the buffalo on the outside of the nickel. When I relate this observation to Kirk, he reels back in horror, baring his teeth:

"Baba would throw up if he knew you were hung up on a

chick like that. She looks like one of those wax dolls that melt in some old fucker's attic."

"I guess so," I say, afraid to defend her because of my status in the Aces. Last week I went to the Lair for the first time, and made a bad impression on two of the greasy members by cutting a book riff. After I had mentioned how I kind of liked Hemingway, a little Ace with no teeth came up to me and said, "You're a smart son of a bitch, aren't you." My head began to loll around on my shoulders, like the spring Gino Marchetti doll in the back seat of Father's auto. Baba came to my rescue, however, by retelling the tale Walter and I had told him about our adventures with the night watchman. Our version was less colorful than the real thing, but made us seem like efficient killers, which made a hit with the gang. Still, I am in a difficult position with the Aces. If they were to find out I am going to cut the meeting this Saturday to take Susan to the movies, it would mean something terrible—like the Bumjar. No one says exactly what the Bumjar is, but I do know that it is the Aces' method for dealing with informers and discipline cases. I fear the Bumjar.

But I am in love. Warm flushes appear on my face at odd hours. My hair is being washed every day, by me. When she sways by me in the hall and says "Hi, Baaaab," I have to run into the men's room and piss. I am having terrible daydreams about myself. In one I wear a tuxedo, have a Cuban cigar clenched between leering teeth and live in a huge mansion with a yard full of white fountains. When I am on the phone with her, my voice suddenly sounds like Sidney Greenstreet, something I cannot understand. Sidney Greenstreet was a fat eunuch who never scored with chicks, and I don't want to sound like him, but that's how it comes out and I am forced to go on with it. She asks me if I am a member of a secret gang, and Sidney tells her yes. I immediately try to take it back but it's too late. For hours I bite my lip and wonder how she has managed to hypnotize me. I fear her worse than the Aces, and can defy neither of them.

On Saturday night, I am horrified beyond belief. All my organs are shaking inside my body. I feel like my lungs are being filled with a green slime, which will not drown me, but will not let me breathe either. I am certain that my heart will pop from beneath my pink button-down and roll up the street. (I imagine massive embarrassment as I beg her pardon to go chase it.) On my way to her house, I wish that a drunk might veer off the road and strike me down, or that a gang of queers would stuff me into their trunk and take me to some decadent address in New York. I am certain that the Aces are watching me with telescopic lenses, and I even conjecture that they may have beaten Susan senseless by the time I arrive. Actually, I tell myself, everything is going to be all right. Kirk thinks I am visiting my dying grandmother in Texas. He was much too excited about going to the meeting to suspect anything. Yet, in the deepest part of me, I know that he knows I am lying, that I am going out with Susan. I pray that he will not tip off the Aces.

As I approach Charles Street, my entire body is a mass of swarming bugs. I look at my hands and imagine them curling like last year's leaves. On the front porch of Susan's red brick house, my tie comes to life and starts strangling me. I grasp it violently, hoping to save myself. Mrs. King opens the door and I try the Sidney Greenstreet out on her. It comes out falsetto. I begin to think of myself as the Flub-a-dub, a puppet on "Howdy Doody," who is half duck and a third ostrich. As I enter the dining room (having no idea what words are being spoken, having seen none of the furniture), fat Mrs. King hands me a ukulele and tells me that when the young men came to see her "way back in the stone ages, ahaha," they always played the uke and sang old favorites. I say that's nice, but I don't know any old favorites. She says oh yes you do. I say now wait a minute. She grits her teeth, snatches the uke and plays madly. I am forced to sing along, wishing I were with the Aces. If only I could catch Mrs. King in a parking lot after PTA. There would be much pain involved.

Many minutes later, after two full choruses of "In the Evening by the Moonlight," Susan appears. She has on a simple brown skirt, a mohair sweater and a huge tiara on her head. She looks exactly like a queen. I tell her that fact in my deepest voice, and she looks at her mother as if I am crazy. I want to hide under the couch, refusing to come out unless coaxed by a nice lady doctor, who understands how badly I've been traumatized. We finally say good-bye to Mrs. King, who tells me she wishes Mr. King weren't in the hospital with cancer so he could meet me. I smile and say that's nice.

Getting away from Mrs. King brings back some of my confidence. I decide that we are going to see the double feature at the Rex, *The Creature from the Black Lagoon* and *Return of the Creature*. Susan pouts and says she wants to see *Tammy and the Bachelor*. I tell her no, that's impossible. I have never missed a horror movie in the past five years, and this is the last night for *The Creature*. She counters by telling me that she read a story in *Photoplay* about Debbie Reynolds and how this movie is a real challenge to her acting ability, how she even had to do a serious love scene in it. I say no again, this time in my own voice. I explain to her the social significance of the Creature. I tell her to look on him as bestial man, man without social hang-ups, and thus man who must be destroyed. When I turn to look at her this time, I am pleased to see her blue eyes wide open, spelling "I love you, I love you" beneath moist lashes.

At the ticket booth I destroy the confidence I have built up by pulling out my plastic wallet. It is a souvenir from the trash heap I played in on the Hill, and has raised pictures of boots and saddles on it. Susan turns her head and gives one short snort of disgust. I bite my lips and ask for two children's tickets. Susan gasps and chokes and I change the request to two adult tickets. She raises her eyebrows, looking forty-five, and asks if I think she is a child. I say of course not, didn't I already call you a queen?

Inside the dark theater, I see rats scamper into the wall. This is nothing new. In fact, we (Kirk, Walter and I, and how I hate to be reminded of them, knowing that they must certainly have squealed) always come here specifically to watch for them. Susan asks what *that* was (as a fat one crawls by) and I say squirrels. She makes another noise, this one less threatening. I place my hand on her shoulder. She sighs.

As soon as we sit down, I slip my arm around her, mentioning what pains I have from a lacrosse injury (actually my arm does hurt, from where the night watchman bit me). Susan does not curl up to me, but leans out of the seat in the opposite direction. I take this as a sign of her decency and character. I am proud she will not let me bully her into a sexual encounter. Suddenly, I have a very great urge to ask her to go steady with me. I picture myself slaving in the frozen food department of the Acme market, trying to save enough to take her on a blissful honeymoon to Acapulco. I have to piss badly.

When I cannot stand the pressure in my thighs any longer, I ask her if she would like to come to the back and wait for me while I go to the bathroom. Before she can react to that, I skillfully rephrase the question to would you like to come back and have a Coke while I go sit on the toilet. I feel that it is important she know I am not going back there to fool around.

After we get a Coke, I sit back and watch *The Creature from the Black Lagoon*. In a matter of seconds he has emerged from the slimy depths and is ravaging a swamp, killing animals, people, upsetting boats, terrifying Julia Adams, playing havoc with bland Richard Denning. I fall in love with his sad, primitive eyes, his lithe muscular body. I want to have his scales, want to take Susan, as he has taken pale Julia Adams, down down to my undersea . . . *Wait wait*—I suddenly understand what is being done to people. White men have made the Creature from their own projection of the blacks. Yes, there is no doubt. The Creature is Negro Man. Of course, yes, taking Julia Adams to his underwater ghetto. I am panicked. It's a plot, a plot. I must warn Susan, I must tell her what hidden dangers exist, they are out to burn her beautiful brain. I grab her shoulders, turn her face to my own. . . .

Bumjar   Bumjar   Bumjar   Bumjar   Bumjar   Bumjar

Oh no. It's not happening here. Oh yes, it is. That cold blue scream, coming from every corner of the theater. I turn, try to hide my head in her breasts. Here come Baba, Kirk, Walter and other screeching Aces up every aisle. No hope. None. They are pushing over the seats, coming at me, still screaming. I try to leap away, and fall into a little old man and his grandson, out to share this Saturday movie.

"Get offa my sonny," says the little old man.

I run into the aisle, Susan's needle shriek a terrifying counterpoint to the ravaged Ace voices. They swoop down on me, tackle my legs, twist my flailing arms. They are carrying me out the exit door, still yelling   *Bumjar   Bumjar   Bumjar*. I am not screaming, not making one sound. I have quit resisting. This is my punishment. I shall take it like an Ace.

Now we are running down the street, fast, faster. Baba Looie has one leg, Kirk the other. Walter is holding my right arm, and an unknown Ace digs his fingernails into my bleeding wrist. Behind us I hear Susan wailing like an injured animal. I am surprised that Baba can move this fast, and I ask him what's the hurry? I explain that I will readily submit to the punishment, that there is no need to carry me at top speed. Nobody answers. Then I see why. In front of us, less than twenty feet away, is a parking meter. They are opening my legs, heading directly at the post.

"Jesus God, oh no," I shout.

Time is coming apart. Creature snagged by wiry net. Reels running backward. Whammmmmmmmmmmmmmmmmmmmmmmmmmmmmmmmmmmm is not an adequate description of the sound. My balls hit the steel at ten miles per hour. The red VIOLATION sign is the last image.

XV.
The Teddy Bear Caper

I am down Ocean City, Maryland, with Randy. My mother has come with us, much to my disgust. It is no laughing matter to be thinking about "making out" (maybe even "getting tit" or "touching a box") with the knowledge that Freda could pop up in her blazing red muumuu talking about what artistic vibrations she gets off the waves. What is more, I am not in the best mental shape. Since my abortive attempt to be a juvenile delinquent, I have suffered the trauma of not being high school fraternity stuff (along with Walter—we were both turned down for Phi Pi), and also a religious-sexual crisis (which will be explained later, because it means more later or maybe to give it the fullest possible dramatic effect). Therefore, I am not any too confident with girls. And I can expect no help from Randy, who stands helplessly by me, wearing his father's green "Alligator" shirt (Dacron with a little alligator over the tit). The shirt has ugly ribbed stuff around the shoulders (the kind old old men wear, sweat white and smelly in the afternoon). Also he has on red chino bermudas, white socks with red and green rings around the top, and black shoes. Randy is even more out of it than the "young people" who come to Ocean City from Lancaster, Pennsylvania. Lancaster is known as the Chicken Capital of the East, and the boys and girls wear powder blue shirts with pictures of the Road Runner on them, or with white letters that spell "Olympic Drinking Champion" or "World's Greatest Lover." Yes, Randy and I have fallen so low that these people look at us and think we are weird.

Not that I am weird. I just feel that way. Weird and kind of bottomless, as if I might be a loser all my days. To fight this malaise, I march Randy and myself up to a fat man in front of a spinning wheel. The fat man looks horribly greasy, as if someone had dipped his skin in french fry oil, and for a second I fear that he will grab me and smother my cheeks with his own. When I pull away, I will have terrible facial gacks, and will be forever shunned by golden girls of the beach.

"I am going to whip this game," I say to Randy.

"Boy I know you is. Boy oh boy I jes know it. You gonna beat thet thar game."

"Silence," I say, holding up my hand.

I then tell the fat man that I will place my twenty-five cents on nine in the red. He verifies what Randy said about me being a natural winner, but I am not fooled. It is quite apparent that he is trying to "suck me in," something he could never do.

"Just roll 'em," I say.

And roll them he does, around and around, and though I would never admit it to Randy, I am very concerned with winning. It's a matter of attitude, like Johnny Unitas says. If

62

you win at one thing you will win at all others. But if you lose
. . . and I know all about losing. As the wheel spins I imagine
myself in a lonely truck stop, rouge on my face and long bony
hands wrapped pathetically around a picture of my son, who
has been killed in the Argonne forest.

"Look at you," says Warren. "You are Bette Davis."

"Shit too," I say, praying that the wheel will reverse my fate.
And it does. It does. Marvelous, weird beauty . . . *I am
indeed a winner. It's true, ah true.*

"How 'bout that," says the greaser. "A winner on the first
time. How 'bout that? You kin have any doll in this row."

He points to a line of teddy bears, green, blue and pink.

"Get thet ole pink bear," says Randy.

"What the hell do I want with a pink bear?"

"You ken give it to Susan. She likes them stuffed animals."

"All right," I say.

The greaser gives me the bear and suggests that I place a lot
of money on the numbers and try to win a bigger bear. I will
not be bullied.

"No dice," I say, instantly feeling lame. My voice is supposed to be commanding, full of fire, but once again I have
only played the jester.

So I stand with Randy on the boardwalk in front of the
giant, creaky Ferris wheel, a pink teddy bear in my hands, and
every second I am feeling less like Errol Flynn. As I fall into
a hot stupor, I see a small, well-built girl moving toward us.
Next to her, miraculously enough, is a fat, woolly-headed
friend.

This is it, I think.

Sure enough the girl walks up to us.

"Hi," she says, tossing her head back and forth.

I won't come on too strong.

"Yeahhhhh . . . yeahhhhh sure . . . I . . . ah . . . see what you mean. Ah . . . hi."

She stares at her girl friend and the fat girl points her chubby finger at her head and makes a circle. I understand that this means I am cracked.

"Hi there, hi ya," says Randy.

I move in front of Randy and squint my eyes.

"What you up to?"

"What you up to?"

"Well . . . I won this bear."

I want to kick myself until I bleed. What a horrible line. But she shows interest.

"Say, he's real neat," she says.

As I hand her the bear, I hear Sam Cooke singing "You Send Me." It's an old record. Sam is already dead. I realize that the record is a bad omen. Then I know why. *The girl doesn't like me at all but is just using me to get to the teddy bear.*

"I'll take the bear," I say gruffly.

I reach out to get it, but she playfully holds it away from me.

"Lemme have it," she says.

"If you don't hand over that bear," I say, "I'll punch you in the tit."

"Big mannnnnnnnnnnn," she says, sticking out her tongue.

I am flooded with misery and know that I am a very sick child. Randy is astonished, and I panic again, thinking that perhaps this exhibition will mean that I lose my power over him. There is nothing to do but go on with it.

"It's the bear or your tit," I say. "All the same to me."

The girl looks at fatso, who does the loony-bird sign again. Then she drops the bear at my feet and runs away, shaking her head.

I look at Randy for signs of rebellion, but in his eyes is unquestioning obedience.

"I guess I told her," I say.

"Yeah, you sure did. Boy you tole her good."

Feeling exhausted and ridiculous, I walk next to Randy down the boardwalk, two robots fried by the sun.

XVI.
Let's Hear It for the Mayor

"Why do I suffer so?" I ask Warren as we begin to march down the long aisles toward the podium. It's high school graduation night at the Fifth Regiment Armory. Somewhere in front of me are Walter and Kirk, dressed like me, in tuxedos. Out in the audience are Glenn and Freda. Right before we left home they had a huge argument about who had sacrificed the most to send me through school. It ended with Glenn screaming that Freda had kept him from being an artist, and Freda screaming that she was going to hire a private detective to follow him day and night. Glenn answered that by suggesting she go to Africa to find Ronald Hogan. Freda threw her hands over her face and Glenn retired to the bathroom to dab creams on his acne and read *I Lived Through Auschwitz*.

But now we are moving steadily, slowly, like some great exhausted snake, through the smoky gloom of the armory. It's

66

the largest graduating class in the history of the school, and we have sat through unbelievable speeches by the heads of state. On the stage, far away, is a red-faced man in a gray suit. He is the mayor and his hands must be getting tired.

But no tireder than myself. What next? College? I have a choice between the University of Maryland and Towson State Teachers College. Naturally my parents are divided on the schools. To spite them, I imagine myself going around the world, traveling to foreign ports, marrying the daughter of a sultan. I will come back in a few years and with me will be a whole horde of Nubian slaves. But the fantasy does me little good. As we ooze toward the stage and our diplomas, I enter the Town to see what's happening. Warren is dressed like a buccaneer and is on the town green practicing swordsmanship.

"Warren," I say again, "why do I suffer so much?"

"You?" He makes a few passes at the air and sits on a log. I cannot see his face well, but I think it's a composite.

"You? What about Glenn and Freda's suffering? You think they don't suffer a thousand times worse than you?"

"But I can't help their suffering. What can I do to end my own?"

"You need solidarity. You must give up your childish violence and kiddie anarchism, and marry Susan."

The idea snaps me back into the armory. I am a hundred yards from the stage, and the mayor is hazy in the lights, smiling, bending over to pick up yet another pink-ribboned scroll. At this moment I feel strange, airy. I'm having a religious conversion.

"Susan," I mumble to myself. "Yes. That's it."

An idiot grin cracks my face, and I nod my head as I ramble.

"Yes. It's clear what I need to do. Give up trying to be one of the boys. Give up absurd, childish dreams. I will find salvation through the love of a good woman. Through sacrifice. No

67

more will I give in to infantile gratification. No, it's through devotion to duty. Just like Albert Schweitzer, whom Susan loves so much. No more absurdity. No more idiocy. I will get a job, any job, and have Susan home waiting for me, smiling at the blinds. I will make meaning for myself. When I stumble in the door she will hand me a drink. I will drop my hat on the couch and hand her roses. We will dance to the music of Broadway and flitter like butterflies across chairs, tables, studio couches."

Though I have never worn a hat, and despise Broadway show tunes, I instantly convince myself that marriage and devotion is my one chance for salvation. By the time I walk across the stage to accept my diploma, I am beaming and puffing my chest out.

"Congratulations," says the mayor.

I stare into his puffy red eyes, but do not see greed. I see, rather, a man of substance, a man of the community. I see a man, like myself, who recognizes the need for duty, fatherhood and all of civilization. God, I love the mayor. I love all the decent little people who sacrifice their own desires to keep the wheels turning.

"Mayor," I say, my voice cracking, "how can I tell you what this moment means to me?"

He looks surprised, clears his throat.

"I am happy for you, son," he says, handing me the diploma with his left hand and crossing over his right to shake mine.

"You are?" I gasp. I am dumbfounded, flooded with love. The mayor loves me. The mayor cares. I drop open my mouth, spread my tender arms.

"Mayor," I scream, "you are mine."

"Agh," he yells as I pounce on him.

"Agh, agh," he says. But it's no use. I love him. I really love the mayor. I'm hugging him. Kissing him. Licking his well-powdered ear. I am out of my mind with happiness. God love us all. God love our civil servants. From the audience I can hear a loud roar, a kind of tumult reserved only for Johnny Unitas when he has launched another touchdown pass. I know that this time the applause is for me, for my new love of the world, and most of all for that greatest of all good men, the mayor.

"You have showed me the way, Mayor," I scream as some officials pull at me and start to drag me off the stage.

"Thank you, thank you," I say, blowing kisses as they carry me down the aisle toward Glenn and Freda. At last, at last, I'm on the true path.

XVII.
Those Wedding Bells

We are married in the Methodist Church. Kirk is the best man. Much crying and my parents slap me on the back. As we leave the church door, Freda kisses my head and starts to tell me about her own wedding, and how she wished it had been the missionary. I tell her that she should see the light like I did. I have completely convinced myself that society is good, that Susan, with her Albert Schweitzer and her knitting, is the answer to my prayers. We have no honeymoon because I am determined to be practical. Our marriage night is spent fixing up our little apartment. It's in a development called McBoyce Manor. The area used to be a garbage dump but is now a filled-in lot with many weeds and few trees. Up the street is another development. Its name is Dutch City and all the apartments look like little windmills. Susan wanted to move in there but I said no, we must be like the mayor, hard-working and practical. She sighs. The sigh continues for a week. It's a small sigh, but steady. When we go to bed the sigh continues but increases in volume. I try to ignore it. I get a job managing a record store, and take night courses in business administration at Towson State. Susan stays home and pretties up the apartment. But she keeps sighing.

"Susan," I say one night, "what about this perpetual sigh of yours? Do you think there is anything you could do for it?"

"Ah-ennhhhhhhh," she says.

"O.K., Susan," I say, kissing her forehead. "You sigh all you want."

Things go on like this for a year. The faces on the record jackets keep changing. First it's folk singers with angelic looks. Then it's folk singers with mean looks. I play one of these. It's a bluegrass record which tells how wonderful it is to bum around the country. I wonder if the mayor ever bummed around. I ask Susan. She sighs. The sigh is very long, more like a yawn. I listen to these new sounds in the morning as she fixes my breakfast, and in the afternoon when I come home for lunch.

"Well, Susan," I say, smiling, "what's for lunch?"

"Ennnnhhhhhhhhhhhhhhhaaaaaaaaaaaaahhhhhhhhh," she says. It's like an airplane going into a nose dive.

"Susan," I say, "you realize your sighs have evolved into yawns."

At the record store I ask for a raise. The boss yawns. I wonder if he has been seeing Susan. Perhaps there is an epidemic of sighing-yawning going around. I shake my head and stare at the happy faces of the people on the record albums.

In the second year, things take a turn for the worse.

Susan combines the sigh with the yawn.

"Susan," I say, "let's quit our jobs and bum around the country like the people who make records."

Her answer? "Ahhhhhhhhhhhhhhhh-ennnnnnhhhhhhh-ahh-hhhhhh-ennnnhhhhh."

"Hmmmmmmm," I say. Then I get scared. I have been saying a lot of things like hmmmmmmm lately. Could I be getting the virus? I run off to the record store and play a bunch of albums.

In the third year Susan does not move at all. She sits in front of the window and stares at her hands. Occasionally she utters a sound, but it is a strange use of language. "Coke," she will say. Or "Cheeseburger." I get panicky and call in a doctor. He comes. A little short man with bad teeth. He stares into her throat. He keeps staring. I wonder if he is considering taking Susan's last asset, her beautiful teeth, and putting them in his own mouth.

"So?" he says. "What's wrong?"

"What do you mean, what's wrong? She only sighs and yawns."

"So? This is perfectly normal."

"Hmmmmmmm," I say.

The doctor gets into his big black car and leaves.

"I think I am going to get some milk," I say.

"The draft will get you," she says.

"You know I am leaving," I say.

"Of course I do. I'm such a bore."

"Maybe it could be different," I say.

"Ennnnnnnnhhhhhhhhhhhh," she says.

Too late. She's fallen back into it. But she is right about one thing. The draft could get me. Still, I have to go.

I leave her most of our money and ride all the way across town to Kirk and Walter's apartment. I have not seen them for two years because of my effort to emulate the mayor.

"Ward," Walter yells as I walk into their apartment.

"Mr. Straight," yells Kirk.

72

"I am going on the road," I say. "Like the singers on folk and rock albums. There is something new happening all over America. Everyplace but here. It's happiness. You all coming?"

"Sure," they shout. We slam our arms around each other and I know that I will never be like the mayor. In the back of my mind Warren is chuckling loudly.

"Just wait," he says. "Wait till you see what else."

XVIII.
Hittin' That Hard and Dusty Trail

We hitchhike to the Baltimore Beltway, laughing and singing. It's six o'clock at night and we have just eaten a huge meal. Soon it grows dark, and we are standing under the arc lights whistling a tune.

We are still under the arc lights, still waiting on the Beltway. Unlike most hoboes, however, we are not being blinded by the cruel neon. That is because the lights have gone out about two hours ago. It's eight-thirty in the morning and we are dirty and exhausted. I am feeling less and less like Woody Guthrie. Kirk is going through an agony routine (falling in the grass, yelling "Oh no, nooooo, pleeeeeeeease pick us up"). Walter is sleeping on his feet, a trick he swears he learned from a Cisco Houston record. I'm still standing here with my thumb out. It occurs to me that perhaps gypsies don't take as many bags as we have. Kirk has two suitcases and a guitar. Walter has one suitcase and a pet hamster named Dusty Roads (he named it as we got to the Beltway). I have two suitcases, a banjo, a guitar, a mandolin, and a camera (so I can take action pictures of us working in the fields with the real people of the earth).

"Ward," whines Walter, "are we ever gonna get picked up?"

"Not unless an empty U-Haul comes by. Look at all this stuff we brought. Nobody in the world would stop for us."

We all look at it. Kirk begins to laugh at Dusty Roads. Walter gets hurt and picks up his belongings.

"I am through. Screw you guys."

Walter is walking up the ramp, kicking his feet into the curb, enjoying Kirk's apologies.

"Come back here. I was only putting you on. I love your goddamned hamster. Christ, I would protect him with my life."

Walter keeps walking away from him, his head bowed. I believe he really is hurt. Kirk tells me he will be right back, and runs after him. I watch them disappear around the bend, my thumb still drooping toward the highway. At that moment two cars stop to pick me up. I race toward the second one, bags and instruments in hand, and explain how sorry I am I cannot go with him but the other guy stopped first. He says I am breaking his heart. I am falling over my suitcases, breaking banjo strings, my camera bouncing in my mouth. With the driver's assistance, I flop into his car.

As I zoom away, I see Kirk and Walter coming back down the hill. They wave good-bye, pick up their things and head back to Baltimore. It's me all alone now, and I am tempted to ask the driver to stop the car because I think he has a flat tire. When he does, I will run away and get back to Susan in time for supper and sighs. But I don't say anything, just watch the highway, hum "I Been Doin' Some Hard Travelin'" and occasionally bite my wrist.

PART TWO

XIX.

In Which the Narrator Becomes a Mountain Man and Harvests the Grapes of Wrath

I am standing barefoot in the soil. (As soon as the first driver let me out of the car, I took off my workman's boots and casually tossed them aside. I also opened my workshirt and imagined myself on a record album, standing on this long, lonesome road.) There are trees firmly rooted in this, the earth. I lean over backward, my banjo bouncing off my knee, my guitar, camera and mandolin dangling from my neck, cutting off circulation. I stare into the West Virginia night, out into the vast vast stars. There is a feeling of absolute elation here (caused by either a mystical oneness with the universe or dizziness from blood shortage), an emotion which begins at orgasm level, travels through the brain, out the top of the head, and swirls into the cosmos from wherever it came. This feeling, this priceless feeling, which lasts three minutes. Then I am forced to admit that I am hung up here, Nowhere, U.S.A., with a bunch of instruments I do not play. I am glad

I do not have Dusty Roads with me, for I would eat him.

"You are a fool," says Warren.

"Monday morning quarterback," I retort.

"Why don't you sit down on the edge of the picturesque country road and shout the blues?" asks Warren.

I do not answer. There is very little I can say that will be classified as fast repartee. I scout the roadside for woodchucks and other animals I have seen in Walt Disney movies. Nothing . . . I put my hands over my eyes (shading them from the moon?) and look on down the line. For as far as I can see (about ten yards) there is only darkness. It is a darkness which has a life, a will; of that I am certain. First it gets black, total blackness. Then it gets blacker. I decide that colors have been poorly named, that if I live through this, I will start a revolution in aesthetics and language by renaming all shades of black, blue . . . This fantasy keeps me from biting my wrist and giving over to unmanly hysterical whimpering, for maybe thirty seconds. Then I feel my lip doing the trembles.

I am saved from an early breakdown by the headlights in the road. Leaping directly into the path of the vehicle (never considering that the car may be doing more than ten miles an hour, thus necessitating my death), I wave my arms and yell, "Howdy, neighbor." Woody Guthrie said in his autobiography, *Bound for Glory*, that all "hill folk" would instinctively understand "Howdy, neighbor" and invite you in for corn bread and sour mash. The car, however, cannot hope to stop and honks its tinny horn once, as it veers to avoid hitting me. I watch it fishtail, spin and crash into the trees a few inches to my right.

"Gee," I yell, as I run over to the smoking battered heap. I am thinking that if I revert to the language of an innocent child, whoever gets out will not turn me over to the Ku Klux Klan for castration.

"Whad the fug you doing in the road?" says a youthful voice, coming from the twisted front end.

"In the road? Gee," I say, two or three octaves higher than usual. I worry that I may sound like a punk and he will cut off my balls without waiting for the Klan.

"That's rot," the voice says. "*In the folking road.* Either you're in the road or omma nigger avaider."

I decide to humor him. He is, after all, a savage, and I should be able to get him on my kind of time.

"Sure am sorry, neighbor," I say, doubling over and making an awkward bow of apology. (I am attempting to look like a humble hill folk who has just won the Congressional Medal of Honor, and is having his reception with the President.)

The ruse works beautifully. He is stopped short by my passivity. I picture myself with flowers around my neck, and all the greasers in the world paying me constant homage.

"Gawsh" is all he can conjure.

"I was jes wandering out on the road, and the darkness made me kinda dizzy," I say. "Om plumb tuckered out."

"I reckon you can stay up at my place for the night," he says, as he inspects the crunched smoking mass wedged in between two fat trees.

"Why, thanks, neighbor," I say, sticking a blade of grass between my teeth. "My name's Bobby . . . Bobbyward." I pronounce both names at once, like Walter Brennan, who is the only hillbilly I've ever seen. It works like a charm. His face opens in a smile.

"Stump's mine. Byron Coughing Bird Stump. You mighta heard some of ma records. You play all them instruments dangling round your neck?"

81

I stare down at my guitar, mandolin, banjo, and camera overwhelmed with embarrassment. The only song I can play is the first verse of "Blowin' in the Wind," and worse than that, the man in front of me is one of the major bluegrass gospel ethnics on the exciting new country scene. Walter has all the In The Field recordings of the Singing Stump Family. I feel like running into the woods and never coming out until I can play all the instruments. But this is not possible, for I would be eaten by bad animals.

"Kinda," I say, still affecting my folksy voice but with a Henry Aldrich falsetto. "I can kinda play 'em."

Before I know what is happening I am in the Stump Family's living room. Two-hundred-year-old mandolins hang from the wall, next to a drooping elk's head, and directly above a silver satin pillow with a picture of a bee with boxing gloves on and a pugnacious look on his round face. Coughing Bird explains to me that the pillow was sent by his brother Tommy Joe, who was in the Seabees but who was "runned over by the only Caterpillar tractor on Guam. Bones jes crushed all up." Five-hundred-year-old dulcimers sit next to the ancient rocker all covered with handmade crazy quilt. The Stumps are glad-handing me. Many backslaps are going down, and I am being pummeled by Daddy Stump, whose real name is Lester Buddy-Bob Stump. I am being hugged by Coughing Bird's cute cute sister (in miniskirt with white tassels and whiter plastic miniboots), Rosie June Bug Stump. I am being kissed (slobbered on actually) by Ma Lottie Stump, and even Coughing Bird is punching at me like an old lost friend. My own reaction is the appropriate "Aw shucks" routine, and I am making as much effort as possible to stick out my front teeth. I decide right then that I am going to spend the rest of my life with these people and cultivate myself as a raucous hick.

82

After a wonderful night's sleep on the softest featherbed in the world (softer than the carpet of grass Johnny U. races to the protective pocket on), I awake to the sound of twanging banjos, booma booma bass runs and blissful four-part harmony. Christ, I tell myself, they sing when they get out of bed. What wonderful wonderful people. I throw on my socks and my workshirt and skip down the ancient steps. Sure enough, there they are in the living room. All of them standing in a line, all of them wearing their green satin shirts with *Stump Family* written across the chest in gold letters. I notice the incredible pair of tits possessed by June Bug, tits which swell with pride every time she strains for a high note. I thrill to the amazing hands of Coughing Bird on banjo, and the equally deft fingers of Lester Buddy-Bob on guitar. Ma is playing Jew's harp in the corner, and is putting down some very hot licks. I nod my head in appreciation, and feel country magic surging through all my organs.

The Stumps are more than grateful for my applause, and invite me to eat breakfast with them. I marvel at the simplicity of the meal. Although the grits gag me, I eat two full helpings of them, and drink three glasses of buttermilk, which causes my entire throat to move inside my neck. But the strangeness of the food (for surely that is all it is: I am learning new ways and new food; real food fresh from the farm is strange to me because I am used to plastic food from the Food Fair) is more than compensated for by the earnest simplicity of the talk.

Pa Stump: "Ah pass them grits and ah gimme them biskits."

Ma Stump (scratching a sore on her nose): "Uh O.K. Here's the vittels."

Pa Stump (rubbing his chin, which is now covered by a long hanging buttermilk loogie): "Boy's gotta ead."

Coughing Bird (grits falling from his mouth): "Ahh umm ahh."

June Bug (wiping her nose with her sleeve): "My nose has an ole bug in it."

I listen to this talk as if it is the first conversation in the history of man. Here are people, I tell myself, who sit down and eat. Really eat. The very *eatness* of the scene is what gets to me. They feel their food, they swish it around in their mouths, let it drop back on their plates. And their conversation reveals the simple joy, lost for all time to the bourgeoisie, of the real *eating process*. I am so overwhelmed by my insight that I forget I may throw up all over this shredded lace tablecloth.

"You *really eat*," I scream. "You *really fucking eat*."

My joy is short-lived, for Lester Buddy-Bob smacks me in the teeth with the back of his massive hand.

I cannot believe it as I fall to the rug, and he is on top of me, beating my face. The other Stumps manage to pull him off. As Ma Lottie waddles to the kitchen to get a cold cloth for the big gash in my forehead, June Bug explains to me that I should "hadn't never said bad words 'cause Lester jes loses his good sense when he hears 'em." I try to explain that the source of the words was joy, that they are the greatest eaters I have ever seen, but it is to no avail. They look down on me with vacant stares and wide smiles of mindless sympathy. I curse myself for my lack of discretion, and spend the rest of the day, working out back in the sawmill with Byron, trying to explain. He tells me "jes to forget it, and maybe Lester will." I say "I sure hope so" many times, and shake my damaged head for emphasis.

That night at dinner, I am not so amazed at the eating process. I am too up-tight to notice anything. Lester spends much of the time shooting me hard looks, and the family ignores me. I swallow my food with great difficulty (this happens every time I get upset, ever since Freda force-fed me her egg and asparagus specialty in front of all my friends on my seventh birthday) and vow to find a way to appease them. During dessert (pig knuckle pie) I tell Lester that he is the greatest banjo player in the world. This does me little good because Lester plays guitar. He raises his hand and tries to give me a karate chop to the windpipe. Fortunately he telegraphs the swipe and I am able to duck. The hand hits my temple, and I am suddenly moving through a dark place in slow motion. Spinning out of the black is a voice, two or three voices, a choir of voices. I awake to find the Singing Stump Family in front of me, their red chubby faces smiling, their necks straining toward heaven. " 'There is a fountain all filled with blood . . .' "

I listen with rapt attention, absolutely bent on winning their favor. Obviously I have broken an unspoken unwritten law of the hill folk, but I am certain I will be able to get back in their good graces.

"That's great," I shout, attempting to applaud. I am unable to do so, for they have me tied to a chair.

"You folks has got me all wrong," I say, in panic.

The family doesn't seem to hear me, and launches into "From Mother's Arms to Korea," a song with the refrain:

> They sent her an unfinished diary
> That told of the life of her son
> It started the day that he went away
> And ended 'neath the enemy's gun. . . .

Finally the family moves in a song I have never heard before (or since) about a man "who skinned a nigger good, boys":

Skinned that nigger good now, boys
Cut that coon rot fine
Twist his balls all round his neck
Stuck 'em in turpentine, yeah

I attempt to show my appreciation of the joke, but am cut short by Coughing Bird, who comes over and unties me. The family smiles a lot and offers me some "home brew," which I drink gratefully. (They do not mention the tying up and neither do I. I figure that some things are better off unspoken.) Soon we are sitting on the crashing back porch, sipping white lightning in the orange moonlight. I realize that the family has some shortcomings, but now that I am being accepted, now that I have at last atoned for my conduct, I am only too glad to overlook these frailties. It makes them more human, I say to myself, as the liquor makes me instantly stoned.

"You know," I hear myself say, with total horror, "for the salt of the earth, you motherfuckers act mighty strange."

I do not attempt to resist as both Lester and Byron smash their fists on the top of my head. In the heat of the morning I awake and stare at the soft pink sky. No, not the sky; it moves. I am underneath a hog, and he is beginning to defecate. As I make futile attempts to squeeze out from under the *big load* I hear the good Stump Family begin a rousing version of "Couldn't Rinky Ramble."

"Ha ha, you bastards," I scream, shaking my fist, wiping hog shit from my eyelids. "Ha ha, ha ha hahahahahahaha . . ."

Though I am covered with bruises and small bits of hog shit (which have dried in the sun), I am determined to earn the respect and friendship of these marvelous Stumps. That is why I am carrying eighty-pound sacks of sugar and shelled corn up the side of this treacherous mountain to the ramshackle still which bubbles merrily beneath the trees. The work is back-breaking and my arms are breaking out in little red spots (from the sun? from anxiety?), but on my fourth trip down the hill, Lester gave me a big smile and handed me a thick crust of brown bread, which was covered with a lumpy red substance. I accepted it, smiling, and experienced (for a second) good moments shared with a friend. Even though it was virtually impossible to swallow (I found myself gagging and rolling over and over in the dust), I must admit that if judged by taste alone, it was quite delicious. After helping me to my knees, Lester explained that it is an old family recipe, a recipe rarely sampled by strangers. It is called chicken beak jam. Through watering eyes and streaming nose, I informed him that I was afraid that one of the beaks had become lodged in my throat. He only said "Haw," and explained that the Stumps never had that trouble because their throats had stretched from singing all those years. I said that I thought they were wonderful singers, and after several minutes' more retching, carried the sack up the mountain.

Now I climb the rickety log ladder up the side of the rusted caldron, and hold the bulky sack of corn above my head. I am suffering from vertigo and a bad case of the sweats and picture myself falling into the steaming mire. However, from some-place deep inside of me comes a new will, a second wind, and I watch the corn fall into the bubbles like a landslide of yellow snow. Then I go to the rim of the mountain and pick up the gigantic ax. On my first stroke I miss the entire pile of wood and slice a worm in two. After burying him (to show my reverence for all living things) and wiping the rest of it on my pants, I again attempt to chop the wood. As I raise my arms, pictures of Paul Bunyan and his Mighty Blue Ox, Babe, are flashing in my mind. I see myself sailing down a snow-banked river with the two of them, a Swiss accordion in Paul's giant red hands, a joyful glint in his eye. The ax comes down cleanly on the wood, but bounces off and springs from my hands, scaring a family of feeding birds three feet away. I lope casually after it, my hands in my pockets, whistling, as if I know perfectly well what I am doing.

"Goddamn birds bother a man," I say in perfect West Virginia twang.

I soon acquire the knack of splitting logs and find myself falling into a regular rhythm. Splinters are flying into the blue air, bouncing off the green leaves. Only one or two sail back at me, digging into my cheeks. I feel new muscles in my body, feel all my organs pumping new, clean life. I pretend the Stumps have made a circle around me and are humming warm-hearted lusty lumberjack songs. Soon I have made a huge pile of planks, and I race to the dying fire. I throw them on, and imagine an instant blaze. Of course, this does not happen, and I remember my Boy Scout training and laugh heartily at the irony of the situation. The very thing I despised is now coming back to me as a blessing. Before breaking up the smaller twigs to place under the massive pile of logs, I stare into the sky, feeling very religious, transparent and glowing with wonder. Without saying it, I am certain (suddenly) that nothing is ever wasted, that somehow everything is connected (beyond good and evil). I light the small twigs and stand over the fire, watching first one, then several of my logs go up in glorious flames. I hear the slow wonderful sounds of the bubbling still, and then a sound from the bottom of the mountain. It is the Stumps, in the backyard, doing a jingling jangling version of "Orange Blossom Special." I see more logs go into red darting flames, and know that tonight we will sit in the back porch sipping our liquor, watching our West Virginia moon. In the morning I will be riding in their buckboard (though I have never seen one on the farm) on my way to some church social, girl friend June Bug bouncing her bustle on my ragged happy knees. I clasp my hands together ecstatically and race to the log pile. Chopping furiously (in time to the Stumps' masterful music), I obtain many pieces of wood. Back at the roaring fire, I dump them on and watch them evolve into huge licking flames. Licking my lower lip, I see myself and the Stumps at the Grand Ole Opry, fifteen thousand rednecks worshiping us with backslaps and handshakes. The fire is roaring now, flames shooting up the sides of the caldron, bubbling going on louder than the Stumps down below. I watch and think I will soon have the greatest bunch of moonshine ever created (and in the shortest time on record).

"It's all happening," I scream into the orange woods.

Then there is a whiteness over everything. And a roar. The roar of ten thousand West Virginia mountain lions after being shot by Lester's carbine. All the roars of all the Colt fans throughout the universe. My happiness reaches some new, indefinable peak as I am carried through the air, whipped through tendrils and woodflowers, smashed into a burning tree. Good Lord almighty, the still has blown to hell.

XX.

In Which the Narrator Meets the Phantom of Cleveland and Learns That There Is No Business Like Show Business

I am wobbly in the dusk of Interstate 90. At my back is a monstrous Allstate sign, which warns me that I should take care of loved ones. Ahead, spread out like a newer and uglier Baltimore, is Cleveland, Ohio. I am highly disappointed that the sun is not shining, for in my dreams I picture Cleveland as a place flooded with light. I have imagined light streaming down on all the good Cleveland mothers as they hang out their wash. I have pictured the wash itself getting whiter and whiter, setting spacious backyards all aglow. This is not the case, and I am sorrier for it.

"Cheer up," says Warren. "Cleveland could not be worse than those wonderful good-natured rustics the Stumps."

"Mockery is a cheap art," I answer.

"If you hadn't left behind all your musical instruments, you could compose a folk ballad to the home of Luke Easter," says Warren.

"I have never been an Indian fan, as you well know," I say, but with little conviction.

"Put out your thumb, stupid ass," says Warren.

I heed Warren's advice and stick my thumb into the smoky air. Within seconds, a Falcon of undistinguishable color slams on its brakes. I race the few yards to my ride, and imagine a camera catching all the boyish joyfulness on my face.

The driver of the filthy vehicle is the ugliest person in the world. He introduces himself to me (with no attempt to shake hands) as the Phantom. For several minutes I am unaware of what he is saying (and he is talking constantly) because I am so amazed at his face. It is longer than Plastic Man's and as red as a Mott's apple. The redness is caused by raised welts the size of silver dollars. His eyes are gray and rimmed by many thousand blackheads, which look like the fantails stitched on Mother Freda's bedcovers. His teeth are big and jaggy and there seem to be too many of them for his mouth. When he grits them together he looks very much like a werewolf. The hair is also wonderful. Massive brown ringlets which fall over his forehead in a Bill Haley loop-de-loop.

After I am awakened from my daze by the spittle which flies from his crooked mouth, I am able to hear his voice. It sounds like Wallace Beery, or the voice of Fernando Roush as he plans some deadly strategy.

"You into this thing, man? You dig?"

"Dig what?" I say meekly.

"Film, man, and revolution. Come on."

"I saw a good movie before I left Baltimore."

He lifts his top lip and gives me an early Elvis snarl.

"A good moooo-vie? I'm talking about revolution, man, not some Lana Turner epic. I am talking about things like acid, and getting your head into something. What are you hitching for, man, if it's not to find that?"

I start to say "That's a good question, buddy boy," but stop myself, thus avoiding an onslaught of bile.

"Yeah, I see what you mean, man," I say, dropping my voice an octave and rubbing my chin. I figure if I act hip, he will not throw me out of the car. But I am also intrigued by this grotesque Phantom. I realize that my entire life is going to go through a major change, and shake my head as he shakes his.

I wait for the Phantom to tell me more important things, but he grows silent. His long red fingers rub around the steering wheel and he leans toward the windshield, like an old motorist driving an antique Packard. In front of us, the traffic has grown thick, and I stare out the window at a Big Boy Family Restaurant. The giant plaster Big Boy wears red-and-white-checkered overalls and stands on one foot. I imagine that he has to go to the bathroom, and picture a balloon over his head which says "I'll give you a free Big Boy Burger if you will stand here a few minutes while I piss." I am about to tell the Phantom of my remarkable insight, but he beats me to the punch.

"Dig that, man," he shouts.

"What?"

"Down there, on the side road."

I stare past his hideous head and see a shady suburban road with many oak trees. About one block down the road is a small crowd. They form a semicircle around what looks like a fallen pedestrian.

"Someone's been hit," I say, feeling excited. I know that the Phantom will not let this situation go unattended.

"Yeah," he says dreamily. His bunny eyes squinch up and he frantically turns the wheel to the left.

"We're going to see about this, man," he says. "Yeah . . ."

We cross the highway, barely missing a tragic accident with an ice cream man, and speed toward the scene.

Once there, Phantom leaps from the car as if his seat were a trampoline. He bounds toward the circle and I leap out after him. I do a perfect imitation of his kangaroo walk.

Lying in the middle of this circle of citizens is a big Negro lady. Her flesh-tinted hose are all twisted around her fat legs, and she is moaning softly. Blood pours from her ears and makes a small puddle on the white street. To my left is a golden car with the title "Cougar" on its side. Sitting behind the leather steering wheel is a skinny girl who is holding her head in her hands. She is moaning many things, most of which are incomprehensible. The only one I am able to hear clearly is "Whoa no, don't die. Oh pleeeease don't die." Phantom has circled the entire crowd like a dangerous wildcat. He bounces up to me, his wide teeth in a yellow grin.

"This is it, man. Do you see it? This is it. That black chick is going to die right here in Cleveland, Ohio, and these people are going to watch."

Phantom then sees the lady in the Cougar and leans in the window.

"You can't believe you are in this, right?"

The lady takes her hands from her face and stares blankly at Phantom.

"You can't believe all this is happening to you, isn't that correct?"

The lady nods, biting her lower lip.

"You were doing just fine up till now, weren't you? You had finally gotten through analysis, and you were just starting an affair with a dentist, and you have just gotten your whole load of Cannon dish towels in the mail, and at night you were thinking about taking French, and for the first time in ages the

93

flowers have sprouted and you owe it all to Scott fertilizer, and now it's all ruined because you had to go and run down a nigger."

The lady tries to say something, but all that comes out are small animal noises. She shakes uncontrollably (much like Mr. Pensy before one of his window attempts) and rolls up the window.

Phantom gives a triumphant laugh and races into the center of the circle. He props the injured lady's head up and tells her consoling things:

"You ain't gonna die, miss. It's all right now."

His tone is just moralistic enough to assure her she will soon be in the grave.

Now Phantom spins into action. He walks over to a businessman in a gray suit:

"Say, baby, that's a nice suit. Looks like gray moss hangin' off an old wall. I'll bet your cock looks jes like that too."

The man does nothing.

Then Phantom races back to the victim, pulls a handkerchief out of her mouth and dabs the blood away from her eyes and mouth.

"Yeah, moss man. You must have a beauty of a cock. Like some great dead fruit. I'd love to have a photo of it. Hang it next to my bowling trophies."

Moss man angers at this and yells at Phantom:

"You better watch your step, boy. This is Ohio."

He steps forward, but a little guy in Bermuda shorts grabs his arm.

"Get off, George," says moss man. "This boy is gonna get it."

"Nothing is ever decided by violence," says George.

Phantom jumps up again and points his finger at George.

"Listen here, you. If I hear any more of this pacifist bullshit

94

out of you, I am going to break each of your chickenshit fingers individually."

George shakes his head sorrowfully, and Phantom reaches between the lady's legs and picks up a rock. He misses George but hits a small girl in Catholic high school dress, with a Saint Vincent's emblem over the breast.

"Hey, watch it," she yells.

"You watch it," says Phantom. "This ain't no crab feast or beer party."

"Just what is it then?" she says, giving him a saucy look.

"If it was up your ass you'd know what it was," says Phantom.

"That's not nice to talk like that," says a motherly looking lady with a gnarled ear. "It's not nice for two reasons. One is that she's a little girl you're talking to, and another is that you might upset the nigger."

"I'm sorry about your ear," says Phantom, "I'm really sorry. In fact, I'll bet you suffer more than anyone in the world. I'll bet all your organs are going bad at once. So why doncha just lope on home and pull 'em out? Yeah, that's right, pull out all those festering organs and roll 'em down the street. Have a contest. See which one can get to the mayor's office first."

"A Communist. He's a Communist. A Red."

Two old ladies pick up the chant and mumble "Communist, Communist" through dry gums.

"Hey, that's nice, Grandma," says Phantom as he motions to me to come in the circle with him. "I'll tell you what. You can have a contest too. Sure. I got one special for you. A sweater contest. You get all the grannies out on the porch some night when you could catch a death a chill, and see which one can wear the most sweaters. I got an aunt who can wear fourteen. You top that?"

95

At this moment the injured lady is beginning to cry and wail. I suggest to Phantom (softly, for fear that he will turn his wrath on me) that it might be a good idea to get these people to do something.

"Yeah, baby. You are absolutely right. While I been rapping she ain't getting any better, is she? Man, I hate these people so fucking much I just lost sight of what we are doing here."

The victim then says she wants to see "Jeezkris" and Phantom tells her that that particular gentleman is not available and that she will have to schedule an interview.

"Hey, come on, Phantom," I say. "You shouldn't bait the lady like that."

"Bullshit, baby. We are all racists, all of us, and it's better to joke about it than let it stay inside. This is a black woman, man. A housecleaner. You gotta admit it, man, you look down on her."

"But, Phantom, the point is that if you don't get these morons moving, this lady is going to die."

"Yeah," he says, shaking his head. "Yeah, I see what you mean. O.K., baby, watch this."

Then Phantom is whirling around the circle telling everyone what to do in a clipped military accent.

"You," he says, pointing to a kid with a basketball in his hand. "Thot's rot, you, lad. Fetch me some water. . . .

"And I say, Mrs. Driver, I say, be a good girl and ring up the ambulance. . . .

"And you over there, wot ho? I say, thot's dandy—yes, you cretins over there. Get yourselves together and bring some blankets. . . . Very good. Very very good."

"That's a fine imitation," I say to Phantom after he has discharged everyone to their proper place. "Why, they don't even seem mad at you anymore."

Phantom smiles. "Of course they're not mad. They can't

sustain any fucking emotions long enough to be mad. They are cattle, baby. Cattle, and ripe for the picking. Wait till you see what I give 'em for the grand finale."

The crowd is beginning to come back. Moss man is carrying three blankets (one of them electric; a nice gesture but a bit much). Half ear is carrying a first-aid kit. The little Catholic girl is carrying a magazine called *Beauty Hints*, which she offers to the victim. (Victim moans.) The old woman brings a huge pitcher of lemonade with gray hairs floating on the top.

Phantom thanks them heartily and places the gifts around the victim.

"Miss Rosie thanks you from the bottom of her heart," he says.

"And while you were going to get these . . . these sweet mementos, Miss Rosie said that there is one more thing she would appreciate before she goes into the big closet in the sky. Yes, she has one last request of you white folks, and she wishes you could grant it, yes, she wishes that with all her heart. And fortunately, my friends, my farmer friends out here in the heartland of this great country, yes, fortunately we have the power to grant her that request. Doesn't it make you feel good? Answer yes, children."

"Yess," moans the crowd.

"Well, here is that last request, good neighbors. Miss Rosie wants you to send her out the way she came in—with a hymn —her favorite hymn. Can we sing that hymn, O children of the plains?"

"Oh yessssss."

"Then gather round. Yes, gather round now. Gather round this woman who cleaned your houses and who you will see no more. Send her off the way she would like best. Show her that you do really care. In your deepest heart of hearts. In your way down real red white blue souls. Show her."

97

The circle gathers round. Moss man unclenches his fist. Half ear and the little Catholic girl embrace. The old women make gummy noises. I move up next to Phantom, who has his hands clasped on his chest. Slowly, majestically he begins:

> Oh it's just a closer walk with thee (Lawd Lawd)
> And it's blessed Jesus if you please (Oh Lawd)
> And it's daily walkin' close to thee
> Ah none but thee, dear Lord,
> None but thee . . .

I open my eyes (Phantom's are closed tightly) and watch the pink open mouths, the straining throats. There are many tears here. Many chills throughout the body. The victim's moans are all but drowned out by the magnificent, swelling harmonies. Yes, these are people truly together, deeply aroused by their own voices, and I watch them kneeling and humming, gathered here together in Cleveland. Yes, oh, we are here, all of us . . . and we stay that way until the baboon cry of the ambulance breaks into our song.

XXI.
The Spirit of Saint Louis

When Phantom and I pull into his girl friend's house in Saint Louis I am gagging and choking. Ever since I slept with the hogs at the Stumps' I have been feeling shaky. Phantom's girl, a tall blonde named Sally Carderelli, is very sympathetic and takes me to a back room, where I crash on a mattress. (Up until this moment, I have not used words like "crash," thinking them too self-consciously hip, but since traveling with Phantom, it seems only natural. All of a sudden I am part of a big movement.)

The day is cool and there are spaces between the floorboards. Therefore, my chest and shoulders get cold and my cough worse. Soon I am half knocked out, and feel as though I am still in the speeding car, next to Phantom. In my head I see his teeth, and bad skin, and behind it is an intense orange light. I begin to think of the Phantom as some sort of con man saint, the kind I have read about in sentimental books about roguish heroes. If Phantom were not hideous, he could be Errol Flynn. Whatever he is, I am glad he is with me, for without him I would now be in bad shape. Not that I am in good shape. We are in Saint Louis, me sick, both of us flat broke.

I lie on the cot for a while, half awake, my body alternating between fever and chills. In the other room there is some kind of party going on. Occasionally I hear Phantom's voice rise above the crowd:

"Yeah, ah, I tink we could do dat ting fo you, man. . . ."

"Sure, he's very bad. Killed a cop in New York for layin' a parkin' ticket on him."

I wonder who Phantom is referring to, and decide it is just one of the many revolutionary people he knows throughout the country. "Revolution." A beautiful word. Yes, I'm on the move, never looking back, side by side with Phantom, I am the revolution.

"Now if you'll jes lay the bread on us, me and my partner could, ah, cop the keys for you and meet you back here tomorrow."

Suddenly I realize that Phantom is attempting to make some kind of deal for us. In a few minutes he comes loping into the bedroom, parading around my bed like some old vaudeville hoofer.

"So beautiful, baby. Jes like I said, God takes care of the strong. The weak, man, gonna fend for themselves."

"What's up, Phantom?" I say, feeling like the sidekick in any old Western you'd want to name.

"Well, out here in the other room, baby, is this cat from some school, Saint Louis University or somewheres, and he wants to cop some grass, you dig. Well, I got him going through such changes you wouldn't believe, you would not believe."

Phantom runs over to the mirror and stares at himself. He pouts out his lips like Mick Jagger and nods menacingly.

"Yep, it's here," he says. "It's officially here."

"The revolution?" I say, propping myself on one arm.

"The revolution," he says.

The next morning Phantom wakes me with the news that I am on my own until two-thirty. Then I am to meet him back at the house. I ask him to explain what is going to happen, but he only smiles and slams me on the back.

"You'll see then, man. Go somewhere. Meet a chick. Just be here at two-thirty."

"I won't hang you up," I say, glad I can use a hip phrase.

"Oh, and here, take this."

Phantom hands me a bottle of pink liquid with the name Robitussin—AC on the label. He tells me not to pay any attention whatsoever to the instructions but to drink half the bottle.

"Half?" I say.

"Not enough?" he asks. "Then drink the whole bottle."

Then Phantom and Sally are running out to her car, and I am left alone with my cough syrup. For a second I hesitate, but then I picture Baba Looie shooting up heroin and feel absurd.

"Hell, I've got a bad cough anyway," I say, drinking the entire bottle.

About an hour later I am sitting in Gaslight Square. My entire body is flashing happiness. Though I have lost all motor coordination, it makes very little difference. I feel wonderful.

"Now I'm really into some good shit," I mumble.

Soon a girl with long brown hair, a lean wolflike face and

101

a fantastic body sits down across from me. I immediately tell her my philosophy of Doorways, which I just figured out.

"Hey, baby," I say, sounding exactly like the Phantom. "You wanna know where something's at? Well, it's like alleys, see. . . ." I pause here as I receive another incredible rush from the codeine. "Anyways, there are these doors . . . and, ah, like some people open the doors and some stand on the other side, just staring at the knocker, always terrified to leave the room they're in, 'cause maybe . . ." I pause again here, because my mouth is so dry I can barely articulate. "Well, so, chickee, ah . . . maybe the room these people are in is like filled with TV sets and bottles of Scotch, so they are afraid to leave . . . but finally . . ."

After I go on in this revolutionary vein for several minutes, I lose track of what I am talking about. My hands are so numb that when I move them I fear they will jerk spasmodically. I am completely wasted.

But apparently Linda Herowitz is impressed. Breathlessly she informs me that she is Jewish and that she goes to Washington University in Saint Louis, which is the Harvard of the Midwest.

"Oh, yeah," I say, nodding out. "I dig . . . you go to Harvard."

"No, silly, not Harvard. Washington U.—the Harvard of the Midwest."

"Groovy," I say, spitting on myself.

"Would you like some coffee?"

"Sure, that's a gas. . . ."

Then she buys me something called Irish coffee, with whipped cream on the top. When I pick it up, the topping falls in my lap. When I make no effort to wipe it off, she comes around the table with a napkin and does it for me.

"You're just the kind of guy I've been looking for," she says.

"Oh?"

"Yes, you're strong."

"Strong." I realize that mindlessly repeating what she says is not the sharpest way to make a hit, but I am unable to do anything else. My eyelids close and my elbow falls off the table.

"You look tired," she says. "What you need is a corned beef sandwich."

"Corned leaf," I say, rubbing my hands across my forehead.

"Beef . . . for energy, silly."

"Beef."

"You are strong." She puts her hand on mine.

I would like to comment on this, but suddenly there is corned beef in my mouth and I have forgotten how to swallow. When I open my mouth corned beef falls down my shirt. I grab my collar and stare at her with great seriousness. The corned beef is incredibly irritating.

"I suppose to you, I mean a person with cosmic consciousness, I'm just one more hung-up Jew chick."

I reach down the front of my shirt in search of the corned beef. The anxiety level is rising, ruining both the taste of the food and my high. I have a great desire to retreat to my imaginary world and take insulin for the rest of my life.

"Next you'll ask me if I've taken acid," she says. There is a big ball of unchewed corned beef in my mouth, which I am too down to chew.

"Well, I haven't taken it," she says miserably. At this moment, I open my shirt and let the first ball of sandwich fall on my shoe. Breathing more easily, I start to nod again.

"I guess I could make up some line about my wanting to expand consciousness through study and discipline, instead of fragmenting it with psychedelic drugs," she says, a tear in her eye, "but you wouldn't be taken in by that, would you?"

I decide to throw caution to the winds and put the rest of the sandwich in my mouth. I realize immediately that I have made a grave mistake. Much of the sandwich gets stuck in the back of my throat, impossible to swallow because of the dryness.

"It's no use trying to kid you," says Linda, shaking her head and biting her lip.

I gag.

"I could tell the minute I saw you walking in here, with your sweater flung over your shoulder, that you, to use your own terms, had thrown open all the doors."

I cannot breathe.

She raises her face and looks imploringly into my own.

"Can you teach me how to be free?"

I knew I should never have fooled with drugs.

"I may resist you. But don't pay any attention to me. Think of me as a deranged person who doesn't know how to take care of herself."

"O.K." The corned beef feels as though it has spikes in it.

"Beat me if it takes that."

"O.K., O.K."

"Would you like to smash me right now to start me off?"

"Yeah, anything . . . believe me."

She sticks out her face from her long crane's neck and I draw back my arm. The violence of the gesture causes the corned beef to pop from my mouth. It lands a soggy mess on Linda's shoulder.

"Oh, wonderful," she says after a second's shock. "It's the unexpected, like Zen. A living example of my own neurosis. Oh, you are beautiful, beautiful."

104

She buys me three more corned beef sandwiches and throws me in her Karmann Ghia. All the way home I eat.

At her apartment I become nauseated, but that does not stop her. Her kisses are like small bothersome suction cups on my neck and lower chest. No sooner has she planted one, than she is off whooshing down another. I push her away and stagger around her bleak rooms. Student furniture, one print—a Paul Klee.

"That's a nice print," I say, feeling so nervous I could leap through the window. Someone told me long ago that when you take codeine you should do nothing but lie back. A normally small irritation will become magnified out of all proportion.

"Come here, Bobby."

She is pulling me on her like some kind of sick octopus. Her arms circle around my back and neck with a magnetic power, cutting off all oxygen. She starts pumping me like a machine, chomping on my ear like Elsie, the Borden cow. And all I want to do is lie somewhere and nod out. What am I doing here with this clinging-witch fuck?

"Hold on a minute," I say.

"Don't tell me. You want to teach me some new positions."

"No, I just have to go to the bathroom."

Reluctantly she lets go of my neck, which is burning with pain. I smile at her and look at the tiny hairs sprouting from her chest, dead weeds from Freda's garden. Inside the bathroom, I feel hot flashes and am weak in the knees. I try to puke but it's no go. Bored, I sit on the seat and read her old *Evergreens*. When I peer back into the room, I am happy to see she has fallen asleep, a paperback copy of Erich Fromm lying flat over her thinly haired cunt.

Depressed and feverish, I make my way through bleak Saint

Louis back to Sally's house. When I arrive, there is no one home, and I fall onto the mattress. Before I have rested very long, Phantom is above me.

"Let's split."

"Man, I can't. I'm sick as hell."

A cruel smile comes over Phantom. It is the smile of Jack Palance before he guns down the poor little rebel cowboy in Shane.

"Oh, yes you can," he says. "I just know you can."

I explain to Phantom that I have a serious case of bronchitis, that if I do not rest I will have to go to the hospital. But he does not seem to hear.

"Get up off that bed, partner. We're gonna make some bread. Both of us."

When I attempt to ignore Phantom, he kicks me.

"Phantom," I say, "I thought we were brothers in the revolution."

"We are. I'm saving you from yourself. Get up."

At that he kicks me again. It occurs to me that these are the scenes the sentimental books about the laugh-'em-love-'em rogues leave out. Everyone pays the dues for one man's romantic visions.

"All right, you bastard, I'm coming."

We are standing in front of the spice counter in the Piggly Wiggly Store, shoveling in box after box of oregano. Phantom is howling with delight, beating his chest like Tarzan.

"Get 'em all, baby. All of 'em."

I place the cart under a whole shelf of oregano and knock the boxes into it.

"Phantom, we got enough."

And we are racing through the aisles, whipping up to the cashier, a red-haired girl with one black tooth.

"What's all that oregano, honey?"

"Secret mystification rites," says Phantom.

In the front seat of his car, we are shoveling the stuff into an overnight bag. Hundreds of boxes of oregano at our feet. I am feeling weaker than ever. Phantom looks at me with disapproval. I realize that he does not think I am enjoying this wacky adventure to the proper degree.

"Do you dig what we're doing, man? We are selling these Med students eight pounds of seasoning for three hundred dollars. Dig it. Three hundred dollars."

"Yeah, beautiful."

But I do not feel beautiful. I feel like a middle-class kid playing at criminal. It worries me that I cannot enter into this affair with the same mystical gusto as Phantom, and for the next ten minutes, as we rip open the boxes, I cut many riffs about how what we are doing is just the beginning, how we are going to live violent ecstatic lives no Wasp middle-aged bulge will screw with us we are the spirit of Rimbaud look out we gonna getcha.

By the time we are ready to drive off to swing the deal, I have managed to convince myself that what I am doing is in the same league with the Great Train Robbery.

Phantom is biting his lips. "You know, man, if they catch us it won't be no joke."

It is these words which change my mind for real. What we are doing is shaky. It's shakier than joining the Aces, shakier than taking on Kirk and Walter. I wonder if all revolutionaries feel a pressure in the top of their skulls.

Then I am parking in a one-way alley. I am hunched over the wheel, so scared I am going to burst. Phantom gets out of the car.

"I meet these dudes one block up, man. I throw the package

107

in to them after they give me the bread. Then I'm going to come tearing down here. Be ready."

I nod and take a deep breath. Phantom walks away from the car. It occurs to me that I love this person, this person I call Phantom, who has no apparent home, no connections. He is living on the edge of annihilation, his ass held over the fire.

Behind me I hear a noise. It's a car wanting to get through the alley.

"Move it, buddy."

What will I do? I stare in the rear-view and see a cab driver. If I leave, Phantom is dead. If I don't, and get into a fight, we are both dead. I decide to leave.

"Get that fucking car outa the road."

"All right . . ."

I gun the motor. Then I realize I can pretend the car has stalled.

"Sorry," I yell back. "It's just dead as a doornail."

"Son of a bitch," he yells, racing from his car. "I know what you're doing here. Grabbing off my passengers. You scab thieving sons of bitches . . ."

"No, wait," I say.

He leaps for my door and I slam it in his face. Up the street I hear a great joyful cry:

"I god da money. I god da money."

"Help, quick," I yell, as the cab driver leaps to his feet. In a second he is reaching through the window trying to strangle me. Phantom is skipping down the street, holding the money in the air.

"We did it, man. Let's go."

"Help," I say. The cab driver is twisting my left ear and gouging my eye.

Then Phantom is on the man's back, like a lion gutting his prey.

"Get the car started," he says.

I do not bother to explain to Phantom that it is difficult to get a motor going when your eye is being gouged.

Finally I manage to get the cab driver off me, and Phantom smashes him with a brick.

"I'm glad we got out of that," he says.

"Jesus," I yell. "Look out."

Running down the street behind us are six very angry men. Two of them are carrying shovels and at least one has a butcher knife.

"Go," says Phantom.

I press down on the gas, but nothing happens.

"It's dead."

Phantom smashes the windshield. The howling victims are not ten yards away.

"We've had it," I say. "So long, Phantom."

I put out my hand to shake good-bye, thinking myself very noble not to have forgotten true sentiment in a time of imminent peril.

"You crazy fucker, drive it."

I turn the ignition key and the motor turns over. At this moment the cab driver wakes up and Phantom opens the door on his head. As the door swings closed, an angry student leaps into the front seat. The car shoots out into the traffic at a terrific rate. We have the student in the front seat with us, swinging a club.

"Burn me, will ya?" he says.

Phantom winks at me and makes a fist with his middle knuckle sticking out. With one lightning motion he gives the boy the Royal Nugee. I go into hysterics as we drop him into the street.

XXII.
In Which the Narrator Discovers the Meaning of Art

I am sitting on a grassy hillside overlooking a parking lot in Aspen, Colorado. Three feet away from me is Lily, from Atlanta, Georgia. She is incredibly beautiful, with blue, blue eyes and long blond hair. Her legs are slender and her thighs golden, as golden as those thighs that eluded me down in Ocean City so long ago. We are sipping Dr. Peppers and I am trying to concentrate on what the Phantom told me last night back at the bicycle shop.

"This is it, Bobby. The perfect place for us. The town is loaded with schools for the rich. Writers' schools, film schools and this art colony. You hustle one of 'em and I'll case the others. We get the chicks, cut our riff and burn these bourgeois bastards so easy. Then we make it to the Coast."

When he said this last night back at the bicycle shop, I stared hard at the old axles, chains and burned-out air pumps, and I knew. I knew that I was no longer Bobby Ward, bumbler and fool, but a new man, daring, cool and strange. I could feel the shells of Glenn and Freda, Walter and Kirk slide from my body, and my head went all electric and real. It was the same feeling I got when the Town of Thatched Rooves was working for me as a kid. It seemed, right then, that my partnership with the Phantom had *really* been like the opening of a door, a magic door which led me from the catastrophe of the past into some wild and undiscovered garden that grew inside my organs and bloomed behind my eyes. We sat there, in that abandoned grease pit, and shared the Phantom's grass, and I wanted to leap and dance among those old and useless parts.

But now, with Lily here, and with her breasts rising and dropping as she tells me about her artwork, I don't know.

" 'n' my daddy sent me out here to paint and do my sculptures, you know, and it's been great. I mean, with the mountains, and the sky, and everybody looks so healthy and friendly; why, it's jes the perfect place to work."

I don't want to look at those eyes. I drop my head, run my hand through my hair and see her legs. Goddess. My Queen from the Town of Thatched Rooves. I hate myself for weakness.

"Yeah," I say. "This place is like . . . ah, well, it's like a . . . man, what it is, is like a doorway. You know, your own doorway, you dig, and you've entered the garden . . ."

And she is staring into my eyes as I talk, and long-haired kids are spacing by, right behind us with huge canvases, and the mountains are looming up like gods behind us, and you are not Bobby Ward at all, but a hip hustler, so don't you weaken to this bourgeois bitch and her Southern drawl.

"You have made the leap," I am saying, "the leap from what is passed off as reality down there in Atlanta, and now

111

you should know what you are doing out here is only the beginning of major changes in your head, because . . ."

Now she is squeezing my hand. My God almighty, is it this easy? I don't know what I am saying, pure grass improvisation, but there is no doubt about it, she is squeezing my hand.

The Phantom and I are riding in a jeep down the highway leading out of Aspen. He is driving, and next to him is this little black-haired chick named Gloria. She's from New York, and she goes to Bryn Mawr, and Phantom is laying it on her, riff after riff, about his trip around the world.

"Yeah," he is saying. "There is this place called Tasmania, you dig, Gloria? And they are well aware of spiritual things, very into it, because it's there that I ran into the Theory of Duplication, which is undoubtedly a psychic aid to the spiritual world."

"Yeah," she says, smiling and showing her sharp little teeth.

"And you see," says Phantom, standing up in the front seat, spreading his arms toward the sinking sun, "you see, what it is, is that they realize the death inherent in all material goods and private property, so they have built the 'little ones.' "

And as we turn in toward a grove of aspen trees that are leaning gently in the wind, Phantom grows quiet, until Gloria has to break her cool and ask him what the "little ones" are.

"You aren't hip to them? Listen. They are small statues of everyday things. Like telephones, cars, houses. Little scale-model statues, you dig? And the people of Tasmania place these statues next to the real things and leave them there. Do you dig it?"

Gloria nods her little head furiously, and her hard black eyes are softening. I sit in the back, amazed at the hypnosis.

"So when a guy gets a car in Tasmania, he also gets a little statue of the car with it, and he places them side by side in his straw garage, you see, and so every morning when he's leaving for work, he sees not only the car but the little statue. Now don't you dig it?"

The jeep is pulling up a long, narrow road now, and the mountains are surrounding us, and down below is a five-hundred-foot cliff, and I know that if Phantom requested it, Gloria would throw herself against the rocks.

"But I don't get it," she is saying, as she reaches into her workshirt pocket to get another joint.

Phantom glares at her, cruelly, no quarter given, and Gloria drops her eyes. Then Phantom's own eyes twinkle, and his huge rubber mouth stretches into a grin. The sun bounces off his yellow, jaggy teeth.

"You aren't hip to this? They never covered this in anthropology at Bryn Mawr?"

She can say nothing. I see it in her head. The revisions, the self-doubt, the terror of not being on top of the situation. What would Bryn Mawr do? How about Ashley Montagu?

"So there are these little statues, and every Saturday of every week, the townsfolk bring these statues to the village square and burn them. There's a huge bonfire, and they chant, like this: *O-lay-o-lay-taz-gan-mee-ka-o-lay-o-lay-taz-gan-mee-kay*— which translated means: 'The life of the spirit is the life of creation. What have we but our heart? Death and no permanence in all physical things. Life in the spirit shall seed the garden of the mind.' "

By the time Phantom is finished with the story, Gloria is smiling like a cretin. Her eyes are rolling around in her head and her mouth is hanging open.

"Did you see that, Warren?" I whisper. "The Phantom is a hypnotist."

"I've heard better stories at vacation Bible school," he replies.

But I do not think of the story. I think of myself up here on this cliff, while down below are millions of Glorias all throwing me dollars, dope and leather clothes.

"This is it," I say to Warren as we jump out of the jeep and stare into the endless aspens. "Bobby Ward is on a long, maybe permanent vacation. The Phantom and I will look at all humanity with no compassion."

As we walk around the bend, I feel the wind whistling through all the holes in my head.

When we get back from our ride in the country, I go to the art school to see Lily. My head is full of plans. I imagine she is a racist who would stomp Negroes to death while sipping a lime rickey. I see her on the old plantation dropping a bonbon into her mouth as black people all around her weep and moan. I think how I let her take me in with those blue eyes and cheap perfumes, and my arms go limp in self-loathing.

I rap on her door with heavy, purposeful knocks.

While I am waiting, I imagine her coming to the door all bleary-eyed, without aid of cosmetics. She will slam the door on me, putting one of her racist hands over her face. This will not bother me and it will not keep me out. I will be like Mike Hammer, slamming the door into her, blocking her weak and futile punches. In a few moments, I will have her gauzy negligee torn off and I will bury my barbell penis into her hairy cushion. After I have left her sobbing and helpless, I will rifle her purse and double-dare her to call a shamus.

"Why, Bobby," she says, opening the door. She is dressed in Levi's and a tight-fitting T-shirt. Her breasts push through, begging me to caress them with my lips.

114

"Come in, honey. I have a surprise for you."

I will not be reduced to her own natural clown.

"Don't want no surprises," I mutter from the side of my mouth.

But she has not heard me. No, she has walked through her living room and disappeared around the corner. So much the better. If she is in the bedroom already, she will save me the trouble of carrying her limp body to the bed.

"Here I come," I say.

But halfway through the front room, I am hit with an overwhelming heat. It's suffocating. Worse than the heat of a Baltimore heart-attack summer.

"Whew," I say, pulling a bright-red bandanna from my pocket. I wipe my forehead and the bandanna is completely saturated.

"Don't you mind the heat," she laughs from the bedroom. "It's just all part of my little old artwork."

"Don't worry about me," I say, gasping. "I have never been felled by sunstroke."

Then I turn the corner.

In front of me is Lily. She looks all wavy, blurry. Through the heat waves I can make out a smile and her beautiful brown arm pointing to a giant, red-hot sculpture of a taco! Its shell is brown and it is filled with huge dark-red beans. I move into the glowing room and see oozing red sauce coming off the layer of meat. I am overcome, exhausted, but I will be no pauper to my Queen. I move closer and see the giant crispy lettuce sitting royally on top of the beans and meat. I go crazy over the lettuce. It's shimmering, cool, even in the ovenshell. I want to touch it, but I know she would laugh as I burned. Phantom, Phantom, where are you now? Her smile, her smile, and her legs all glowing. And on top of the lettuce, like a nipple all hard and ecstatic, is a round, succulent black olive.

"Oh," I say, like the woman getting it snappy in the back seat at the drive-in. "Oh, the Big Taco."

And then I am racing out of the room, afraid of what is happening to me. I sweat; my legs buckle. Lily is up on the balcony waving to me, calling my name, and I have failed the Phantom, failed the test again, and I am racing, loplegged, like my father, down the Aspen streets.

I cannot tell Phantom what has happened to me. I cannot stop what is still happening. For two days I sit in the greasy, darkened bicycle shop, smoking grass and looking at my hands shake. I think of Lily, of her smile, so horribly alluring. I think of the steaming, sweating Taco, connected to Lily as surely as her beautiful legs are connected to her crotch. Phantom and Gloria come and go, and stare at me. All I am able to do is spin the old bicycle wheel on its bent axle and nod my goofy head. When Phantom comes back alone, he opens his hand and shows me two hundred dollars.

"And that's only the beginning, baby. There's a whole lot more, you dig? You and me are gonna take a little trip around the world real soon."

"Sure," I say, putting the second cigarette in my mouth like a bad comic. "Sure we are."

"By the way, man. I don't want to hassle you, but haven't you been letting off the pressure on this chick Lily? I mean, she's a gold mine; what ripe pickin's."

"Gold mine," I say. "No fool's gold, that one."

"Right," he says, sitting on the English racer and pedaling fast. "So like why don't you get your ass up there?"

"I feel a little sick," I say.

After Phantom throws me out onto the street, I am shaking

and heaving. I can remember the strange odor of the Taco heat. I can see Lily smiling. I don't want to go. I appeal to Warren. He has left a sign hung on the inside of my ear— "Gone to Mexico." I do not see any humor in the mockery of the sick and injured. If I survive this, I will seek some vicious revenge on that little pest.

I walk the dusty streets of Aspen, past the boutique shops with their paper flowers, nifty wood carvings and cutie-pie names—Mr. Snowman's Cottage, Santa's Reindeer ("Our Clothes Are Endowed with All the Charm of the Old World"), Slalom City. I look in each and every window trying to find something to divert my attention, but soon all the knickknacks begin to pile up in my mind. They are molding themselves, creating something monstrous. I shut my eyes, watching them crawl over one another, little reindeers, baby dolls with big eyes, miniature sleighs, Swiss ice crushers. Portuguese lime squeezers, each of them quainter than the one before; and they are turning brown, and I know they will soon be the Giant Taco, hot, spicy, irresistible. I shake my head very, very hard and race around the corner to the Pure Air Bar and Grill. Inside the window is a fat cook. I stare at him through the glass. He stares back. He smiles. I am positive he will hold up a taco and eight-by-ten glossies of Lily in a skimpy bikini. It is no use. I see it.

"If you were half a man," says Warren, "you would race back up to that crummy artist's colony and attack. A good offense is the best defense."

"Yeah," I say, "yeah. She can't tempt me and get away with it."

I start up the hill, flashing pictures of Johnny Unitas coolly sidestepping the Monsters of the Midway to toss an eighty-yard game-saver to Lenny Moore.

When I am halfway up the hill to my rendezvous with fate,

I see someone racing toward me. It is Lily. I bite my wrist and stand waiting for her with my hands on my hips.

"Bobby, oh, Bobby," she cries, rushing to me with open arms.

"Oh, Bobby, you must help me. You must."

Then I am holding her, feeling those perfect breasts heave against my bony chest. She is sobbing wildly, making animal wails.

"Anything," I hear myself say. "There is nothing I wouldn't do for you."

We sit down on a little bench beneath a great tree. After many pats on the shoulders and three fatherly kisses, she is calm enough to tell me what I must do.

"Oh, Bobby, there is another student at the art colony, nobody knows which one, and he's a thief. He stole sculptures and paintings from three girls last night, and today I got this note."

I take the crumpled piece of paper from her desperate fingers and read:

> You may as well spare yourself an unpleasant and traumatic scene by leaving the TACO masterpiece outside your apartment tonight. The others I have stolen were nothing compared to your sublime creation, and I WILL HAVE IT. There is no force on earth powerful enough to stop me, for FATE has deemed it so.
>
> In deepest admiration,
> Carlos

I crumple the note in my fist and look straight at Lily. She looks back at me, a tear running down her face.

"Who is Carlos?" I say.

"I don't know." She sighs, throwing open her hands.

"An alias."

"Yes."

"He'll never get the Taco. You can count on me. Where is it now?"

"In my room. I left Sarah, a girl friend of mine, with it."

"Can she be trusted?"

Lily begins to cry and throws herself into my lap.

"I don't know. Oh, Bobby, I don't know who to trust."

"Let's go," I say.

In the basement of the art colony I find two leather straps. After thanking Sarah for guarding the prize, I suck in my breath and walk into the sweltering bedroom. Lily hands me a pair of silver gloves and I lean down in front of the sculpture. She pushes it over on my back. I cannot bear the heat. The straps cut into my armpits, and I am thinking of my spine snapping. This will not be easy to explain to a doctor. He will not be able to perform surgery if he is trading Mexican wisecracks with his nursing staff.

We move slowly down the steep path. The heat is overwhelming, and the massive spicy odor makes me reel from side to side. Lily walks in front of me over the stones. I see her hard brown calf muscles contract and loosen at each step. If I push my neck mightily against the fiber-glass shell (but not too mightily, for I fear the synthetic juices will ooze out of it and scald my back), I can lift my head enough to see her frosted blond hair tossing in the breeze. But the heat is overwhelming, and I ask Warren if I should demand that Lily turn off the infrared heater which lies like a steaming rock in the center of the monument. He is being playful with me by answering in lilting, sonorous Spanish. This is a language which I no comprende.

The sun blazes down upon us, and Lily's ass sends off spirals of heat, spirals that are smaller than, but of the same unbearable temperature as, the masterpiece.

119

I cannot bear to stop and turn off the batteries. It is doubtful that I can go on like this.

The hill has ended. We are on level ground, walking down Gold Street, Lily two steps ahead, shimmering. It occurs to me I want her. Right here. Lying on the street, her legs wrapped in ecstasy around my shell. When we reach orgasm, the stuffing will pop from the top of the black olive. I will make the papers, end up with my own show on television, prime time.

The mothers are coming now. They stroll from the exclusive tourist restaurants with their silent, crew-cut husbands. The husbands are bent, but only slightly, from the weight of their children, who are harnessed to their backs. The mothers walk by me first, tanned, thirty-five, with good slender bodies. They smile quickly at Lily and then grin at me. Though it kills me to do so, I push against the shell and look at their white, even teeth. Their eyes do not meet my own, but are locked above my head. I think they understand the Taco very well. Their husbands do not smile at all, but frown, and in one case growl, disapproval. The children take one look and react in the extreme. It is always either hysterical laughter or terrified bawling. I know they think the Taco is my child, some great abomination of nature. Perhaps the mothers think so too.

When I tell the Phantom that we must hide the Taco in the bicycle shop, he shakes his head and mumbles "Ballcutter." However, after I assure him that this inconvenience is but a single thread in the tapestry of my cold-blooded scheme to bilk Lily out of her bankroll, he agrees to go live with Gloria for a week.

I kick away the nuts, bolts, springs and broken handlebar grips from the center of the shop; and we set the great object fully upright. Lily stares at it and throws back her head in laughter.

"Isn't it beautiful?" she cries.

Before I can answer, she is upon me; and with no modesty whatsoever, she is grabbing my hand and placing it on her cunt. I trip over the bicycle pump and nearly crash into *it*. Lily grabs my crotch and we fall on the crummy mattress. I am ripping off her pants and kissing her flat stomach, thighs, burying my head in her bush. Though I am very excited, I cannot resist looking at the Taco. It is glowing red, the whole giant shell. Lily is pulling my head up to her, biting my lips, her hand squeezing my penis. The Taco is erupting molten hot sauce all over old gearshifts and patent leather bicycle seats. Lily is moaning for me to put it in her, and I am certain that the Taco is bubbling an echo to her screams. I jam my cock into her and she wails. We are moving up, down, up, down, and the plastic lettuce is casting unspeakable shadows at frightening speeds. I am going crazy now. Yes. Yes. More intense than Johnny Unitas. Yes. Yes. You can get into my beans. I don't do this for everybody, but you, you're different, and I want you in my beans, throw your cock into my meat, gurgle with my lettuce, spicy on my stomach, and I am coming and you are coming all down the lettuce and all over the beans, and there's them red hot peppers oozing down the bike floor.

We wait for Carlos. I take the morning shift. Lily handles the evening. Aspen is not a large place, and we must be diligent. We both know he is bound to find us sooner or later. The Phantom is getting anxious. Though I wouldn't let him into the shop due to the increasing hideousness of the odors and the staggering death heat, I did talk with him through a small slit in the sliding door.

"Hey, baby, when you gonna make your move? I got all I can get outa Gloria. I want to split for the Coast."

I have been able to stave him off for three days, but I am living on borrowed time.

The days pass slowly. Lily's mascara has been sliding around on her face for the last three or four hours. She was fortunate enough to find a jagged piece of mirror on the floor, and now she spends most of her time holding it in front of her. The last time we made love, I could not breathe because the air has become so heavy with rancid spice. She cried mightily into my lap and I held her dripping, stringy hair. If I were cruel, I would tell you it looked like the broccoli that Mother Freda overcooked.

It is becoming hotter all the time. The plexiglass beans give off a pulsating brown-red glow. The juices of the artificial meat ooze an overripe aroma, which is difficult to assess. Though the lettuce still shimmers, I noticed (after climbing a ladder to survey the situation) that several of the inner pieces are wilted and soggy. I fear the Taco is losing its charm. It is definitely not edible.

"Carlos or no Carlos," I say, staring at the floor, "I can stand the heat no longer. I've got to have air."

Lily is kneeling in front of her creation. In her hands is a large burned-out bean, and over one shoulder is the lettuce.

She is playing her trump card—pathos.

All I know is the odor is making me sick.

Lily has lost her suntan.

There is a knock on the sliding door.

The Phantom stands next to me.

"We have to go," I say to Lily.

"It always ends like this," she replies, cuddling the bean to her cheek.

122

Another cold bean falls to the floor. It rolls toward my feet. I pick it up and hand it to her. But she refuses to accept it.

"Take it as a souvenir," she whispers.

"Did you get the money?" asks Phantom, wheeling away on the English racer.

"No, prick."

"Then fuck you," says Phantom.

He gives me the bird and leaves.

I hire a U-Haul, and Lily and I take the remains of the Taco up the narrow mountain path. It is difficult, but we manage to pull it off. The Taco rolls down through two cedar trees and runs into a black boulder. It is fractured into countless pieces.

The ride back is marked by grief.

"If you are evah in Atlanta . . ." she says, attaching her false eyelashes.

"I may be. I just may be," I say.

We kiss. It's very painful. We kiss again. It's getting dull.

I let her out of the truck and watch her ass shimmying up the rocky hill.

PART THREE

XXIII.

In Which I Arrive in San Francisco and Meet My Queen and My Astral Twin

Now it is San Francisco. I have had three uneventful days, and am entering at night. The hills are all lights. The bridge is burning with brightness. It is Warren and me together, entering this American Wonderland. I am feeling my body move, blinded by the brilliance of the place. In the car, the driver looks at me strangely. I talk to Warren.

"Do you realize what this is, Warren?" I say as we cross the Bay Bridge.

"No. Tell me."

"This is indeed the living Town of Thatched Rooves."

"Don't count on it."

"I count on it, Warren," I say.

"You have been burned before."

"I count on it. I am through liking pain. I am getting out of the movie. I will not be taken in by Phantoms. I will not be taken in by rustic phoniness. I don't believe in mom and dad. And I distrust the whole revolution."

"So where does that put you?" says Warren.

"Out of the car," says the driver, a sophisticated-looking man with French cuffs and three or four wavy strands of hair.

"How come?" I say.

"I don't like people who talk to themselves. It's not healthy."

"I live in a fantasy world to compensate for the absurdity and stupidity of this one," I say, which is the complete truth. Or nearly the complete truth.

"You are crazy then," says the driver, as he pulls off at an exit and lets me out.

"I'm young and I can dance," I say. I jump out the car door and dance on his hood.

He yells, "Hey, hold on there," and jumps out after me. I run down the street, waving good-bye to him, feeling wonder and love surging through me. I am home at last.

And what a home. The home that I have imagined is at once a poor substitute for the reality of the streets. Thousands upon thousands of people wearing all colors. Music in every doorway, sung from pimply lips. Shops selling articles to be found nowhere else in America. It's exotic. It's alive. I skip from person to person, not caring that their faces are filthy. I accept joints from black people who have long since transcended Miss Rosie. Hostility everywhere, but hostility for the right people.

"This is indeed brotherhood," I say to Warren, as I accept an acid tablet from a short boy with more hair than Old Shep.

"That's correct," he says, looking past me, his eyes waiting for a miracle.

"How long has this been here?"

"I don't know, man. I just got here yesterday. You're taking some boss acid, man. Righteous."

"Beautiful," I agree, and think of Walter and Kirk back in ancient Baltimore, walking through gray streets.

"Did you hear the news?" I say. "Baltimore, Maryland, was hit by a bomb, but no one knew it."

"Don't laugh," says the kid, as he brushes the hair out of his eyes and stands with all his weight on one foot, just like the Grateful Dead in the picture above his head.

"Why not?"

"Laughter is lies, man," he says.

"How can that be?" I say, amazed that I have gotten into such a deep philosophical question with someone only three seconds after meeting him.

"Because while you are laughing, your circuits are shortened, you aren't seeing, and what if your Astral Twin came by while this blindness was taking place?"

I start to say "My Who?" but think better of it. I will not be accused of deep probing, the mark of the weakened intellectual. Instead I grunt.

"Uh," I say.

"You dig what I'm talking about, man?" he asks, and disappears into a shop called the Phoenix.

I sit on the curb and finger the blue-dot tablet he has given me. "Acid," I say over and over again. "I am taking acid."

"That makes you a real fucking guru," says Warren.

"Cynics are only failed saints," I answer.

I think about my Astral Twin and look at the feet of those passing by. All the feet seem to be etched with character. All the feet are the feet of Victor Mature in *The Robe*. Sandals with one strap, sandals with two straps, sandals with knee-high straps, toes that ride on the sandals majestically. Toes with the dirt of a million cities, a million miles in them. I remember Mother Freda trying to force me to take baths, bitching about the amount of water I use, and I laugh wickedly. I hold the pill to my eyes and imagine all the wonders of the world seen

129

in it, and then more wonders, wonders which are not seen by the masses, but only by people who have the courage to face them. Beauty so blinding that Glenn's eye sockets would go up in smoke. I assume a hunched-over position, like the boy next to me, and mutter to myself:

"So this is my fate then. To be a carrier of beauty."

I throw the pill down my throat, with no precautions, hoping that an FBI agent sees me. I will transform him into a drop of water and carry him to the Pacific Ocean. Then I will blow the drop to the waves, and he will become like the sea, ever changing yet the same.

Shep is back.

"You drop the acid, my friend?" he says.

"Yes."

"O.K., man. Now let me tell you about Astral Twins."

"Yeah, man, you do dat," I say, dropping my voice to a man-of-the-world huskiness.

"The guidebook says that every person in the world has an Astral Twin, and that if you get your consciousness expanded you can see him. So like I been taking this Owsley shit for three days, standing here waiting for the cat."

"Wow," I say, genuinely excited.

"Yeah," he says, closing his eyes and waving back his hair with a jerk of his head. "And when I find him, I'm going to swing some big deals, you dig?"

"Sure," I say, immediately picking up on the fantasy, which I know is a fantasy but which draws me into it anyway.

"I dig. You can pull some kinda huge deal, make a whole lotta money, and then let your Astral Twin take the rap, fly to South America and start a new life for yourself."

"India," he corrects.

"Yeah, I see. Spend the bread on a palace, study yogi."

"Study what?"

"Yogi," I say, terrified that he has found a chink in my new hip armor. If this were Baltimore and he called me like this I could rap him in the chops, but this is *San Francisco*.

"It's Yoga," he says coolly. "You not some kinda cop, are you?"

"No, I was just testing you," I say, remembering the same stunt pulled by George Raft in *Undercover Man*, when he was nearly found out by a gang of weapon thieves.

"I don't know about you, man," he says, and gets up. "If you're a cop, though, you'll have a bad trip. See you around."

I try once more to convince Shep that I am not a cop, but it's no go. He goes through a beaded curtain in the back part of the Psychedelic Shop, and I imagine him calling out a band of hippie toughs to hurt me. Just as this mind-expanding drug comes on I will be taken out to Golden Gate Park. They will camouflauge my screams by playing rock music through sixteen amplifiers. Then they will circle around me, hitting me with love beads and old sandal straps. I will fall on my knees to show them that I am indeed a religious man, but to no avail. Louder music, and circling hateful hippies, my belching mouth filling with drugs (music louder and *louder*). In the end they will give me an overdose of heroin and leave me in Golden Gate Zoo, lying broken and moaning in the seals' cage. Horrified by this prospect, I immediately head away from Haight Street. Already I can feel my body moving through space, and a definite tingling in my brain. Good Lord, this is a mighty drug I have taken, and I am having paranoid thoughts. This will not do. I decide to sit in the Panhandle, a wide strip of park two blocks down from Haight Street. Once there I will look at the smallest flowers and see all the veins pulsating life, just as the girls in the *Life* magazine articles do. Then I will feel a oneness with nature and get rid of all the hateful impulses which have been programmed into me from a lifetime of hate and fear. Sixteen hours later I will come back to this earth a new man, a man who has earned the right to wear colorful tunics. I will hold my neck back at a tilt like Charlton Heston.

I sit on the faded green park bench, a sprig of some yellow flower in my hand. Actually, I am unable to concentrate on it, because the LSD is sending me out of my body at incredible rates. I can think of nothing, can do nothing. Everything is going around and around. I am afraid I will fall off the bench and break open my skull. Therefore, I use the little presence of mind I have left and lie on the grass. This is much better. Every blade seems to hold precious moisture in it. Every little ant is made up of the finest organs. I hum happily to myself and roll my forehead on the wetness.

"Wonderful," I say. "This is indeed wonderful."

"Give me all your money or I will kill you," a voice says.

I realize that this is just an acid hallucination and feel no fear. In fact, it seems to me that I have come upon a great insight. The mind is like a pie, and one little slice of the pie might be fear, and that is the part that most people feed on. But I will take another slice, the slice of the pie that is full of cherries and wonderful flaky crust, and by eating this piece instead of the moldy old fear piece, I will magically restore the whole pie to its original sweetness.

"If you don't give me that money," says the voice, "you aren't going to believe what's going to happen to you."

I feel a sharp point on my back, and though I am certain it's only a hallucination caused by this consciousness expander, I turn over. Above me is a girl with long hair and a beautiful face. The face of all the stars in the galaxies. The face . . . my Queen from the Town of Thatched Rooves.

"You are my Queen," I say.

132

"You are a dead king unless I get the money, sweetie," she says, smiling.

The knife is at my throat, but I am not afraid. My Queen would do me no harm. This is a test to see if I am brave enough to be worthy of her hand.

"Here is my money, little Queen," I cry, delighted.

I hand her my wallet and see her sprinkle fairy dust all over my body. She says, "Thanks, baby," and disappears into the bushes. I cannot believe she has called me "baby," and pat my own cheeks many times. The grass, however, is a little cold, for she accidentally cut off the buttons on my pants and shirt before leaving.

I stand, shivering, and hold on to my pants. Along Oak Street the cars whiz by at two hundred miles an hour. Several people look out at me and point with great enthusiasm.

"What a wonderful place, this San Francisco," I say.

Then I walk along the edge of the road, listening to the sounds of the engines, hearing the musical honks of the horns. Lights are beacons of friendliness, windows are eyes which look back at me and shine with approval. Two blocks back, on Haight, there is a red glow, the glow of warmth and great fellowship. And now, standing next to me on this corner (which is really a pleasant oasis where the weary travelers stop to refresh) is a huge bus. The door opens, the door to all the caves of Ali Baba, and I ponder the wonder of it.

"Opened all by itself," I say, shaking my sailing head.

"You wanna ged on?" says the bus driver, who looks exactly like Ralph Cramden.

"Oh no," I say, feeling suddenly afraid. What if he takes me back to Baltimore? What if the authorities get hold of me and make me have a choice between ninety-nine years in the pen or being a banker for the rest of my life?

The bus driver shakes his balloon head at me and starts to

133

slam the door. It is at that moment that it happens. I see *him*. Sitting near the back, and staring directly at me, is my *Astral Twin*. Joy shoots all over my body, every pore an orgasm of happiness.

I pound on the door and the driver opens.

"Why didn't you tell me?" I say, ecstatic.

"You want on?" he asks.

"What do you think?" I say, running up the steps, my arms open, embracing the fat sweating driver.

"Of course I want on," I shout. "God almighty I want on."

The driver does not respond warmly to my hugs and kisses, and yells "Fuck off, buddy," but that does not worry me. I race to the back seat and fall on my knees in front of my Astral Twin.

"I've found you, Bobby," I yell. "And on the first trip."

The man makes an attempt to stand but I grab his knees.

"Together we can make a million," I say. "We can change the whole world."

"Who is this nut?" says the man, kicking at my smiling mouth.

"Don't play hard to get," I retort. "Fair's fair, and I have found you. It's in the guidebook."

The man falls on top of me and the bus driver grabs my legs.

"Don't Bumjar me," I yell loudly, as they carry me up the aisle.

"You're my Astral Twin," I scream, as they toss me down the steps of the bus.

"Please come back," I say, drowning in my own tears, as the huge lopsided bus rolls away forever into the San Francisco night.

XXIV.
Poem for My Queen

It is only fitting that I have a Queen. It is only fitting that she wear royal robes, that she be a goddess. Nothing about her must be ordinary. She must speak with the diction of Mab. She must walk with the elegance of a cheetah. She must be a good cook, and must hold my soaking head in her arms after a hard day on the throne.

> Even her urine should be regal. I demand red urine.
> Blood of Queen.
> Even her armpits should be regal. I demand lightning
>   every time she raises her triumphant fist.
> Even her ears should never hold wax.
> I demand a Queen.
> All of the Town is out a-hunting for her.
> For the next several days I will hold auditions.
> In a week I will have my goddess, my love, my Queen.

Warren is behind a curtain, dressed in striped plumage.
He whispers that I am heading for a fall.
Though I am sure he is right, I will never listen.
Palms at my feet. Stars for breakfast.
I am no mean King.

XXV.
Love Among the Liberated

The next day I am on the street. My suitcase has been stolen, and my pants are held together by pins which I stole from a drugstore. I am standing on the corner selling papers called *The Oracle*. In *The Oracle* there are many articles of great interest, such as "How to Get by on the Street." In this article (written by someone with the name Head) the author explains that you should first realize that there are many benefits to living on the street, and these benefits are in exact ratio to the dangers. Head says that without danger life is nothing, which sounds like the Phantom's philosophy, and my own philosophy of Doorways, which I now realize was again the Phantom's philosophy. Anyway, Head goes on to say that living on the street toughens you up, gets you out of many softhearted middle-class death trips. I say Three Cheers for Head. I have always believed this, but if I do not eat soon I might die before I have a chance to toughen up. Head also says that living on the street exposes you to the sun and the rain; in short, forces you to realize Nature. This realization, according to Head, will bring about a lessening of the ego. And when the ego is diminished, then you will be able to see outside yourself and be in touch with the eternal. I agree with Head in principle, but I still wish I had my shoes. Head did not mention the broken glass which is in between every side-walk crack, and which makes painful injections into your soft middle-class feet. Right now I am bleeding profusely. Head finally goes on to say that you get laid a lot on the street, and that the chicks and cats whom you lay will not be anything like Billy and Susie from back in Butte, Montana. I think Head has good intentions here too, but the only girl I tried to start a conversation with barked like a dog and flipped her forefinger on my nose. Head apparently gets to go to bed with Gentle All-Loving Flower Girls, and it is I who must sit here on the street reading his article. I am not certain that if I met him I would care for Head. In fact, I might like to kick Head's head around (like big Lou Michaels kicking the football Sunday at Memorial Stadium in Baltimore). And how I miss Baltimore. Actually this fantasy cheers me up. The very thought of Baltimore gives me renewed faith in San Francisco. Nothing could be worse than Baltimore, with its gray streets, ten thousand Catholics, with its Baba Looie and Kirk, my vicious friends. I grit my teeth and yell "Get your *Oracle*" to cars which are lined up all the way down to Fillmore Street. My luck is not so good, because within ten square feet there are about fifty paper boys. One of them is playing a flute, another is beating on a drum, one girl, who is very small (weighs about forty pounds), is dancing in whirling circles singing, "love, love, buy your love." All of these people are selling papers, and I realize that I must have a gimmick. There-fore I go into the little candy store and with my last quarter buy five Bonomo Turkish Taffys, which I lick and put on my cheeks and forehead.

"Get your papers from the Candy Man," I say. "Candy Man's got all the news."

Immediately windows roll down and hands come out with change.

I imagine myself rolling in wealth. Soon I may even have enough money to buy the Band-Aids needed for my infected toes.

"Candy Man," I yell again, as a willing customer places some change in my gooey hand and insults my decorated face.

"Crazy Candy Man give you mystical *Oracle*," I say.

"What else has the Candy Man got to give?" says someone as she taps me on the shoulder.

"Plenty, baby," I say, without turning around. This time I will not be taken in.

When I do turn around, I make certain to shake the hair out of my eyes and assume an uninterested slouch. I fetch several deep sighs and casually rub my hand over my chin. She is a lean chick, with too much eye makeup, and paint all over her face.

"That candy on your face all you can do, baby?"

I peel the Bonomos off my cheeks, but am unable to get them off my forehead.

"No," I say, sighing and throwing my hair back again; I decide that I do not want to do the latter too often because my hair is just barely long enough to fall into my eyes.

"Can you screw?" she says.

"Yeah, man," I say, so excited I can hardly talk. I'm going to screw a Young Revolutionary. Not a fake hung-up Midwest Jew, but a really freed woman. Still, I manage to outwardly manifest no signs of excitement.

"Come on then," she says.

I make one more mighty effort to pull the taffy off my head, and walk with her down the street. We bob and weave between the thousands of people who are eating loaves of bread, playing guitars, posing for the cameras that are being clicked from the cars lined up in the street, rapping madly at each other about where to cop; actually copping heroin, grass, Methedrine, any drug you want and some you didn't count on (like oregano). She is telling me about how bad the cops have been around here, and how our hippie brothers are being harassed more and more every day (which brings about a feeling of instant indignation in me). And as we turn up Cole Street and walk by a tall skinny motorcycle boy who is putting his foot into the throat of a dog, she begins to tell me about middle-class fucking and how bad it is, how no middle-class people can ever just say they want to satiate their body needs and go fuck but that they have to act like they love one another, and even get married when all they really want is a piece of ass, and soon after the marriage they get tired of each other, and the dumb fuckers really turn her off. Yes, I say, yes, that's the truth, and I do agree with her, but I wish she'd tell me her name; it might put things on a slightly more personal basis. We go into a big white house with brown trim around the windows and a God's Eye hanging in the narrow hallway. She is still raving on about hang-ups, and spins the God's Eye violently.

"That's it, man," she says. "I won't ever stop until I can blow God's mind."

"Yeah," I say, smiling. "That's very poetic." Something is happening here. I don't know what it is exactly but I can feel myself becoming hostile. She is reminding me of something I have seen before, and whatever it is I don't like it.

We climb up the gray dirty stairs and open her door, which is covered with action shots of the Hell's Angels, and she walks directly to her single mattress, pulls off her pants and opens her legs. All the time she is still talking about how little love there really is and how to most men love is this property-ownership kind of thing, and she looks tremendously bored. Then I am balling her, and she is moving up and down mechanically, both her eyes wide open, her mouth sneering at me, and after five minutes I come but she isn't able to.

Then she wants to get on top, and I say O.K., and she tells me that a lot of chicks have to be on the bottom to feel dominated but not her, oh no, and her stringy hair smells so terrible in my face, and she is moving up and down on my cock like a locomotive piston, her face straining and her lips trembling, and I am looking past her to the sink where the dishes are piled up with green fungus hanging off the week-old tacos. Then she screams:

"I can't come. Jesus fucking Christ."

At that moment all the hostility leaves me, and I want to hold her in my arms. But when I try to, she leaps up and screams that she is no Doris Day Barbie Fucking Doll from Butte, Montana, and I know she has been reading Head.

"Wait a minute," I say, as she throws on her Levi's. "It's all right."

I want to make her feel better by telling her about the time I took some amphetamine and my cock shriveled up to the size of a pea, but she won't hear it.

"Sure, tell me some condescending pile of shit. Make baby feel better."

I offer her my arm, but she spits at it and runs out of the apartment.

I shrug my shoulders, smash two of her Donovan albums and go back onto the street.

XXVI.
The Terror of the Swami and Some Speed-Freak Football

Here I am in Love City sitting beneath a big purple flower, unable to do anything. It is a depression worse than finding out I am not a clever con man hustler, worse than finding out the Stumps are brutal morons, worse than being a papier-mâché delinquent. It is all these things combined and more. Yesterday, for example, I sat in this exact same spot watching the freaks go by in their army shirts, blue jeans, robes, ostrich plumes. I read from a handbill advertising Swami Krishnamurti. The bill told me Swami Krishnamurti could penetrate into anyone's real self, make them aware that they were to share this earth with all sentient beings and give them (anyone) the first step toward Total Consciousness. In spite of my bad experience with the Liberated Girl (I saw her again yesterday, whacked out of her skull on Methedrine. She approached me as if we had never met and asked me what it "all meant." I was clever and told her that it "all had two meanings." This bit of nonsense delighted her and she went off with some pimply dude, mumbling, "Two meanings . . . yeah, it's all got two meanings")—in spite of my bad experience, I do not intend to give up my search for the deeper meaning of reality. If there is nothing beyond eat, sleep, spin a disk, ball a chick, get a TV, drop dead on your ass . . . then I will not hesitate to suck in a tubeful of killer gas and let some garbage man find me slumped in a trash can early in the morning.

But I was speaking of yesterday (I feel vague too, incredibly vague, as if someone had thrown a net over my heart). I was happy with the handbill, and the bearded, sagelike face of the Swami convinced me that he must be real. He had the kind of wrinkles that are earned through many years of hard knocks, and a pair of glow-up eyes, which suggested that somehow he had turned every one of those hard knocks into a victory of the spirit. What is more, the handbill looked expensive and the whole thing was sponsored by Resurgence Youth Movement, a group I have heard much about. It is said that RYM takes no shit and cannot be compromised, which sounds good to me. Yes, I sat here yesterday, a day like today, and pictured the Swami staring deep into my soul. He would whisper some strange magical words, and I would walk from the meeting well on my way to Ultimate Knowledge.

It was then that I got the fear. For, as if by magic, the sports page of the *San Francisco Chronicle* appeared at my feet. Without thinking, I picked up the windblown piece of paper, and read this headline:

UNITAS' ARM INJURY MAY END HIS CAREER

The article gave many points of view and all of them agreed that Johnny U. may well be through. Instantly I was struck by a double fear. First, I feared for Johnny U. I felt as if I was losing an organ, an important organ I could not do without.

143

People would notice the departure of the organ, and shake their heads in silent pity. But the deeper fear had to do with the Swami. What would happen if the Swami chanted his chants, burned his incense, lifted his hands above his head, created a fog all over the room, and then in a mocking voice told RYM that my soul was not filled with enlightenment but with dusty, cracked images of a football quarterback. How would that look? I'd try to go to the Fillmore Auditorium and the Jefferson Airplane would stop jamming and make up a satirical song about me. All the pictures from the Light Show would suddenly be of Johnny U. I would run out in the streets, terrified, but the Mime Troupe would be there on a flat truck mercilessly lambasting my bourgeois tendencies. Yes, it is a bad thing to have a hero you cannot shout about. He chokes you from the inside, digs his cleats into your heart.

With these absurd but nonetheless real fears, I get up from my bench and walk past hippie hill. Many long-haired people are passing around joints. I sit down, smoke a licorice-papered joint and feel a little better.

I am learning, I tell myself. I am learning what a mixed-up and fearful person I am, and learning is a painful process, for without pain how do we grow?

These thoughts give me a wonderful buzz in my head. Then I remember that I have just smoked some grass, and think that the thoughts may have less to do with the feeling of enlightenment than the dope, but this does not stop me from having more thoughts, wonderful thoughts about pain and learning:

'Cause Bob Dylan had a motorcycle accident, which caused him pain, and he had to stay in bed for many months and when he got out he wrote tender songs for the first time because he had been close to death and perhaps that is what I am going through, some kind of death . . .

I go farther into the park, walking slow and cool, trying to

144

act as if thousands of freaks all sitting around playing guitars, sitars, vinas, tablas is nothing to me. And when I think of Kirk or Walter back in Baltimore, they somehow look very, very square, and I decide that I will never again admit I am from Baltimore, no, from now on I will simply say "Yeah, ah, like I yam from de, ah, East, you dig?" and people will lower their eyes and think I am from New York. This thought gives me the cramps again. Jesus Christ, I am like some gassy Pinocchio; it's disgusting.

Then comes the weirdest scene of all.

I turn the corner, and see—no, I can't believe it—a hippie football game. It's true. They are out there, about twenty skinny, shirtless long-hairs, running and passing a football.

"Amazing," I say, "it's absolutely amazing. . . ."

Automatically, I drop my shirt on the grass, take off my shoes. In the next second I am in the huddle.

"I'll play quarterback," I say, in an aggressive voice which sounds like Kirk's.

"Sure, man," says a kid who is pulling a little white vial from his pocket.

"What's the play?" says another, lighting a joint.

I watch as the first boy ties himself up and injects the needle into his arm.

"Is that speed?" I ask.

"Yeah."

"Gimme a hit," says a fat boy with wireless spectacles.

Now we sit in the grass, passing around the Methedrine. I feel agitated, and expect the other team to penalize us for delay of the game. But when I look across the scrimmage line, I see there is little fear of a five-yard walk-off. A huge cloud of smoke rises from the defensive huddle.

After shooting up the speed, I realize exactly how to run my team; the out-and-out speed freaks must play end and back-

145

field positions. The pot smokers can be decoy flankers (being too hazy to actually carry the ball) and the heroin junkies will be the forward wall. I have a great urge to make a complex offensive which will combine the single wing, straight T, lonesome end, triple wingback flying wedge all at once simultaneous. Also, I feel like I am being swung around by my heels.

"Unbelievable," I say, falling backward. My head is bursting with whiteness, the wonderful team is here *Yes it's my team and I am the quarterback of my team you aren't quarterback I am quarterback.* Wonderful speed magnanimity and love of life flow through every single pore.

I begin to rap to the boy sitting next to me, incredible fantasies, which begin about football but end up in Tangier with the whole team sitting in ominous opium dens never ever doing a thing. . . .

Finally, I settle down enough to call the play. I get down on my knees and draw a diagram in the dirt, which includes mousetrap blocking, inverted sweeps, fake ball carriers, hidden ball tricks, Statue of Liberty crisscross double reverse whammo handoffs end arounds tackle eligible, three laterals, two crossfield passes and a drop kick, also fake. When I look up from my play, I notice there are few players left.

"Where is my team?" I ask, speeding steadily.

"Who knows, man?" says the fat kid. "You been rapping for half 'n hour."

"I have?"

"Sure, 'n' it was a gas. I'd love to see that play run. It'd be beautiful."

"Let's whip those mothers," I say.

"Are you ready?" I yell over to the other team (three guys left, all of them lying on their backs).

I stand in the backfield. Many thousand fans fill the stands.

The pennants are blowing inside my head, tickling my eyeballs. Loudspeakers strike up the band in every artery.

"Eleventy-two, hike," I yell, the ball spinning to me through the crystal clear San Francisco air, yeah this one for Johnny U., win one for the Gipper, all of this with the utmost importance, 'cause this ain't no mere football contest, this is knights at battle with the dark world, and this is speed power bursting through every minute of time and there is the fat kid downfield, look at that arm of solid muscle, you ever see 'n arm like that and he is way beyond the defenders, this is gonna be touchdown baby touchdown all the way 'cause when your up your up and when your down your down but when your up against speed you haven't got a fuckin' prayer.

I let the ball go with all the might of Zeus flipping his javelin. It sails soars can't believe how far it's going. I sail soar with it, can't believe how fast I'm going, and he catches it, catches it and keeps right on running, right on into the lilac bushes of Golden Gate Park.

XXVII.
In Which an Old Friend Disturbs the Peace

In the peace march down on Market Street, down among the cassette tape recorders, cheap genuine Japanese radios, army socks, midget cameras for taking pictures anywhere nobody sees what you are up to, brown-suited businessmen, there are commitments being made, commitments which mean the end of goofy rebellions, before leaping back into the mother arms of security. No, this is different. I can feel it. There are clenched teeth, and arms folded tightly, and all of them shouting "*Hell no we won't go,*" as the streets flower with young freaky kids all my brothers I think, again whacked out on speed, and grass, "all my brothers," I mumble to Warren inside my head behind my eyes.

"I wish your brothers would let you breathe," he says.

And it's true. I'm packed in here, some fat man's elbow smashing my ribs like popsicle sticks. Yes, these are all my brothers we are gonna change it all electric current of youths

148

out on every street pouring over the world like the paint can picture from Mother Freda's garage studio, pouring over everything, changing the world through love.

Speaking of love, there is this black hair twisting around, floating around directly in front of me, and on the other side of the hair I had a glimpse of the eyes, large, black and deepset. She is wearing this long blue dress, which looks like something Queen Guinevere would have on as the knights gather around the round table in all the dinners at the Town of Thatched Rooves.

"Hell no we won't go . . . Hell no we won't go . . . Hell no we won't go . . ."

The hair in the eyes in front of me, and the man's arm slicing in between the ribs, can't get my breath too good because of the speed, and I feel crummy, dirty, in love with this dark girl.

I watch her move away from me, being pushed by the crowd, who seem to be surging toward the other side of the street.

"They're burning their draft cards," someone says.

A great cheer goes up. It's a brave thing to do. I know I should not be thinking about this girl now, but should be basking in the aura of self-sacrifice, be making some kind of plans to step out of my own skin and figure out what I am going to do when the draft board finds out I am out of school, but there are these eyes, and cheeks so brown. . . .

I push ahead, shove a man nearly on his knees to stay behind her. I must not let her get away.

"Watch where the fuck you're . . ."

I turn my head, making my face all menacing and surly like pictures of the Rolling Stones.

"Tough toenails," I spit out.

Then I feel foolish. I am staring at the Phantom.

"Tough toenails?"

149

"Phantom," I say, as an arm shoves my jaw out of whack.

He smiles and pushes at a man who is sticking a big sandwich into his mouth. An onion or two fall down the man's shirt.

"Phantom, I want that girl up there," I say; it occurs to me that the Phantom will be able to do the impossible. The crowd will open like the Red Sea and I will run to embrace her in slow motion.

"Sure," he says, and starts manhandling people right and left.

I follow close behind him, and in a second I am breathing down on her hair, the blackest, shiniest hair I have ever whiffed.

Phantom is smashed up next to me, trading insults with the sandwich man. The girl turns and stares directly into my face. Her eyes are like almonds, but cloudy, and stoned.

"This is not my bag," she says gently.

"Mine either," I say, looking straight into those eyes. I am so excited that I can barely breathe.

"You need some more mayonnaise on dat sanwich," says Phantom to the man. "You ain't got enough on your chin."

I am smiling at her, trying to think of something to say, and she is staring back. I begin to think how we must look like an advertisement on television, and how all around us the action would fade until only our eyes were left and then over our eyes would come an image of a cake of soap or some deodorant, and that thought nearly ruins this for me, but not quite, for she is smiling now, and saying in a low voice that for a march devoted to peace she has never seen so many people filled with hostility, and bad karma, yes, I am agreeing, feeling like Henry Aldrich as I stare into those fathomless black eyes, swirling pools of water in sunburst Maryland woods. . . .

150

"Hell no we won't go . . . Hell no we won't go . . . Hell no we won't go . . ."

"My name is Mal," she says.

"Mal?"

I put my arm around her to shield her from a fist which is flying past Phantom's head.

"You pig," says Phantom, kicking the man in the shins.

"Hell no we won't go . . . Hell no we won't go . . ."

I watch the man drop his sandwich, yell and reach for his foot.

"Jesus, Phantom," I say. "We gotta get outa here."

"O.K., baby," he says, and starts back the other way.

I am holding Mal's arm, pushing her along. The crowd is growling at us, and Phantom is screaming at them:

"Peace? You want peace? There ain't no peace comin'. Do you dig? The world is all going up in flames, can you dig that? Flames, worldwide rebellion of youth, no more of your comfortable peace marches, can you understand?"

"Your friend is amazing," says Mal in my ear as we follow Phantom.

"Hell no we won't go . . . Hell no we won't go . . . Hell no we won't go . . ."

Then we are running through a gauntlet of store owners, bankers, teachers, who are yelling things at Phantom and he is yelling back, and one old man with white hair, which is blowing wispy off the top of his pink head, is standing in front of Phantom, blocking our path, and he is calling us Fascists, saying that he has seen it all before in the 1930s, and Phantom is telling him that if he doesn't step aside there will be blood all over the dove on the poster in his old hand.

"What the hell are you doing, man?" I say, grabbing Phantom.

151

"There can't be no peace, man. This old dude doesn't understand. Unless we are revolutionaries there can never be any peace."

"Fascists," yells the old man, hitting Phantom with the poster.

I am terrified that this will come to blows and that the whole peace march will come down on us. I don't know what to do.

Then Mal steps between them. She stares first at the old man, and then at Phantom. I watch, amazed and electrified, as she leads Phantom away.

"Beautiful," I say to Warren. "She's stone beautiful."

"Cheap theater," he says, but I don't hear a word, only watch her hips sway as she walks alongside Phantom, her hand gently guiding him away from his private rage.

XXVIII.
A Dinner Debate and the Signs of a Curse

I sit on the grass across from Phantom and Mal. All around us people are ladling out rice soup, eating thick yellow slices of homemade Digger bread. The Diggers are an organization which is trying to feed the "community," and Mal says they are beautiful. Every day she walks up to their big ramshackle house on Page Street, helps boil the soup and beats the dough into shape. Now as we fill our stomachs and listen to a boy named Lizard play a soft, beautiful song called "Country Kites," Phantom tells us we are being deluded.

"Don't you see?" he says, jamming the bread into his hand. "This is bullshit. It's like the peace march, man, pure bullshit. How long do you think this scene can last, man?"

He is looking at me, but I am unable to reply.

"It'll last about six months, maybe a year. Then the hoods will move in, the punks, the commercial scene, and you can kiss Haight-Ashbury good-bye."

"There are ways to prevent that," says Mal softly.

"No way," says Phantom.

He is on his feet now, towering above us.

"Sit down, Phantom," says Mal. There is a tough edge to her voice which surprises me, a huskiness which makes me think of docks, and bars with nets on the wall, and Mal dressed in black mesh stockings and a low-bodiced blouse.

Behind Phantom is the setting sun. It makes a frame for his long head, for his twisting lips.

"Hey, man," he says, "you say something; you got a good head."

"Mal's right," I say. "This is the beginning of a huge thing. It's a spiritual thing."

I don't know why I say this. Perhaps it's to score a few points with Mal. I am so in love with her eyes, clothes, voice, that I am beginning to believe there *could be* a spiritual revolution. On the other hand, no sooner do I say that to myself than I feel like the words came from somewhere else, from some *Time* magazine article on the hip scene.

Now Phantom is roaring.

"Lemme tell you something, man. I was in this flower scene before either of you dudes ever got away from the playpen. I went up to cops and kissed them in Chicago, and got my head stuck in a piss bucket. And in the East Village, in Tompkins Square Park, I seen my chick get her face busted open with the butt end of a riot gun, and you tell me this scene is forever? Hey . . ."

Phantom is so exasperated that he cannot continue. I am deeply moved by his eloquent anger, and want to tell Mal that she is a fool, that because she is a woman she is kidding herself with sentimental ideas about life, about the fact that people can be changed with kisses and flowers. But before I

154

am able to say a word, she has given Phantom and me a deep smile.

"Do you want to hear a torture tale, Phantom?"

We say nothing, but look at her, perfectly composed, her skin relaxed, her earrings tinkling slightly in the wind.

"When I was younger I lived in Dallas. I believed in what all of us believed in—mom, flag and apple pie—only I really believed in it. My father is the vice-president of an oil company and my mother is in the DAR."

We sit quietly, watching Mal turn a flower around in her fingers, listening to her voice, soft and sad, tell us of her love affair with a guy in her father's office. I watch Phantom stare at the ground, biting his huge scarred lips as Mal speaks of her plane trip with the married man. They had gone to New York and stayed in a hotel, and he was going to leave his wife, the oldest story of all time, but she fell for it because she knew she was too smart to fall for the story, it was too obvious and couldn't be happening to her, and all that weekend he showed her off to his slick friends inside a Mercedes-Benz, her mouth on his cock, they would be married, yes, and never go back to Dallas, never. But, of course, they did go back and, of course, she was sick in the plane, feverish and hysterical, and she grabbed the controls and tried to kill both of them, and when he slapped her senseless, she tried to leap out of the plane, all her Bible Belt religion coming back on her in a flood of guilt and twisted broken fragments. And later she would go to sleep and dream of the American flag coming to life, twirling and breathing through the stripes, as it coiled around her neck.

"It sounds funny now," she says, "a flag . . . sounds corny even, but it was what went down for me, it was my own absurd horror, and I was frigid for years because of it. Don't you see?"

"So what's that prove?"

"That proves nothing," says Mal, "but the fact that I now ball and enjoy it, the fact that I am no longer hung up on that experience but can tell it to you like this, means a lot. And what means more than that is I got this way through the Krishna culture."

"Yeah, I dig where those people are at," says Phantom. I am not certain if he is approving or putting them down.

"It's the only way," she says, and then she looks right past us, as if she is no longer trying to convince us of anything, but is communicating with the infinite.

"There is only one way to get out of this culture—through the mind and through the body, through utilizing the godhead which is in all of us—and this is what we must strive for, communion between people on this deepest awakened level. Anything short of this will simply result in new tyrannies, new violence under a new banner, plane trips to New York for all of us, but like it was for me, the city will be ashes. . . ."

I am too tense to eat, and stare at Phantom. He still holds his eyes to the earth. There is an incredible silence, a silence which is at first dramatic, but then spills over into embarrassment, melodrama and disgust. I feel confused, ecstatic. I want to tell them both something that will clarify it once and for all. I begin to speak, but something smacks me in the head.

"What the hell?"

I run my hands through my hair and look on the ground. Lying in a puddle of spilled Kool-Aid is a football.

"You gotta take it back," says a voice.

"What?"

Coming toward me, in rags, is a familiar shape. It is the fat boy I threw the winning pass to in the speed-freak football game.

"What's the big idea?" I say, feeling lame.

"If you don't take the ball back, I'll leap off of Golden Gate Bridge," he says.

"What?"

Phantom is smiling hugely and rubbing his hands together.

"You threw me the ball," says the skinned-up, filthy teammate. "You threw it and I caught it just like you said, and I sat in the bushes all night taking STP, and I knew that your throwing it meant something, meant a curse, a heavy curse, don't you see, and you gotta take it back or I can't get rid of it, you gotta."

"Beat it," says Phantom.

"It's made from the skins of animals, and I caught it," says the end.

"That makes you a killer," says Phantom.

"Take it back. Take it back. *Take it back.* . . ."

Then he is screaming and dancing around in front of us, always keeping his eyes on the football, and I take it from him slowly and put it in my arms, and he asks me if I intend to sneak back into his pad at night and put it in his bed, did I know that it had a microphone in it, that football, and that voices come out of it *You gotta take it back, gotta.* . . .

Mal starts to get up and comfort him, but he pushes her and runs into the bushes, still screaming about the curse.

I flip the ball in the air and stare at Mal and Phantom. We are all certain that this is the beginning of something strange.

XXIX.
In Which the Narrator Is Exposed to the Charms of Howard K. Zucker

I am in the street, peering through the slats of Lucky Red's Bar and Grill. Behind me, in the back seat of the car, are the Feldstars, the Air Kings and the Zircons. Inside the bar, hunched on the stool and talking in low, confidential tones, is the Phantom. He is showing one of the Feldstar watches to a sophisticated-looking middle-aged couple. I don't like the looks of it. The last person we conned with this hustle was a half-drunk workman named Buzzy. When he realized he was going to "get himself a bargain," his huge arms tensed and his breath oozed from his big lips like smog. I liked the smell—stale beer, smoked sausage and pure greed. He gave us twenty dollars and showed the Feldstar off to every other stooge in the place. By the time we left, we had sold three more.

But this time it's going to be difficult. This couple is too well dressed, too sophisticated. Him with his gray hair curling fashionably over his pink ear and his French cuffs twinkling in the hazy light. And her (his wife? his mistress?), all done up in a red and gold miniskirt and big golden earrings. Just seeing them there, under control, no trace of greed on those bland faces, makes me tremble. Just the same, I am not going to bite my wrist; and I am going to do my part.

Now that time has come. After adjusting my red-striped rep tie and dusting off my sport coat (both expertly stolen by Phantom just for this hustle), I walk through the door. Once inside, I move my head in a complete arc, as if hunting for a friend. After moving my head back to its original position, I take a stool at the bar, three down from Phantom.

He is really into his pitch:

"It's like I told you, Howard. These watches fell off a truck. I was just lucky enough to find a few."

Howard's cheeks puff as he smiles. He swishes his drink, puts it to his lips and takes a long sip. The woman smiles and does the same thing. They place their drinks down simultaneously. Howard smiles at her condescendingly. My right leg is doing little nervous hops and sweat is pouring down my forehead. I order a drink from the short, swarthy bartender.

"Let me she . . . see the watch again," says Howard.

Phantom looks over his shoulder as if he can't be too careful and slides the box across the bar. Howard fumbles with it and drops it to the floor.

"Christ, mister," says Phantom, getting up. "You wanta draw the heat?"

Howard says he is sorry and then turns and stares at the woman. Her small face shrivels up as if she has tasted something sour. Then she reaches down to the floor and picks up the box.

"Thank you, my dear," says Howard. He opens the box, takes out the watch and holds it up to the red light.

"Attractive mechanism, highly attractive," he says.

159

I sip my martini and feel better. He is obviously loaded, an easy prey. I am filled with a veritable cornucopia of love and respect for Phantom. He never misses.

"Isn't this a beauty, my dear?" says Howard.

The woman nods her head and smiles weakly. Howard then holds the watch toward me and looks out from behind it.

"Handsome, sir?"

Is he mocking me? I feel panic. I look away, down at my drink, up again at the tropical-fish tank.

"Only one thing," says Howard in an overloud voice, as if he was trying to get my attention.

"The only thing is that I've never heard of a Feldstar."

This is my cue. But I can't respond. A dead giveaway.

Phantom explains that the watch is British and is just being introduced to the States.

Howard smiles and pulls a big wad of bills from his pocket. He orders another drink for the three of them. Is he teasing us? If I ran away now, I could hide out in a mission and eat old doughnuts. I hate my cowardice.

"British, hey?" says Howard, sneering openly now. "Yes, I am a great admirer of the English peoples. We owe them so terribly much."

Again he looks at me. I am going to crap myself.

"But just the same, I never buy something I haven't heard of. It's just not sound business, as they say."

Phantom shrugs.

"All right by me, my man. You don't buy it, some other dude will. I'll catch you later."

Phantom gets up to leave. Thank God. We can go to another bar, start over with dummies.

"Wait," I say. "Is that a real Feldstar?"

I could knife myself. Now I've got to play out the part. All three of them are looking at me. Here comes the martini right up on the walnut bartop.

"Ah, I couldn't help overhearing you," I say in my British voice. Oh, Christ, why did I use that?

Smiling like a madman, I move down the bar, sliding from one stool to the next. On the second one, my legs wrap around it and I almost fall over.

"Ah ha . . . one too many," I laugh, recouping. "Excuse me. Wife tells me not to imbibe; but anyway, my liquor has never interfered with my business sense. I mean, I know a Feldstar when I see one. Do you mind?"

Phantom shrugs again. I think he is overdoing shrugging. He hands me the watch.

I hold it to my ear, twist the minute hand, strap it to my wrist.

"I say, that *is* a Feldstar. How much do you want for it?"

Phantom looks at Howard, begins to laugh bitterly. "What is this?" he says through clenched teeth. "You guys some kinda team or something? Plainclothes scene?"

"Marvelous," says Howard. "Aren't these boys marvelous, Alice?"

"I'll give you fifteen dollars for this watch," I say in falsetto.

"Oh, fifteen, is that all you want?" says Howard. "That is too much. I mean, really. You two went through all this for fifteen lousy bucks?"

He knows. He knew all along. The fat beaver. I feel a sickening panic. Howard will have the big bartender grab us, while he calls the racket squad. I should have stayed in Baltimore and made a home for Susan. Why didn't I capitalize on my educational opportunities? Beatings in the cell. Walls that keep closing. Oh, I am a disgusting bourgeois.

Phantom is smiling, patting Howard on the head. "So you are hip to us, huh?" he says. "Too much."

Howard is doubling over with laughter. He is mocking me: " 'Oh,' " he yells, holding up the watch. " 'A Feldstar, a *real* Feldstar.' That's wonderful, simply marvelous. You boys have made my night. Isn't that right, Alice? I mean, here we were sitting here, drunk and bored, and then you two clowns come along. Really a miracle of timing. Fantastic."

I begin to laugh too. What a pathetic ruse. How could I have ever let Phantom talk me into it?

All of us are at the bar laughing, even Alice.

Suddenly Howard stops laughing. Alice continues. Howard looks at her and I can see their faces in the wall mirror. She is trying to stop, her face is contorted. Howard keeps staring. She stops.

"I'm sorry, Howard; I mean, you were laughing. You told me it was funny."

"Yes, my dear," he says, no trace of a smile on his face. "I did tell you it was funny. And now, my darling, I am telling you that it is not funny. It's not funny at all that these two boys, for that is surely what they are, mere boys, have gotten so destitute of both material wealth and imagination that they feel compelled to try a little trick so banal and absurd as a fake-watch hustle."

Howard turns and stares at us. He is big, fat and slick. I want to hate him, to scream at him, but I feel little, skinny and ridiculous. I wait for some kind of vicious counterattack from Phantom, but one look at his face tells me that he feels the same way I do. Howard looks like a wall that will collapse on us. I want to run out of the bar and call for help.

"So you boys thought that you could fool old Howard with that one, hey? Let me tell you kids something. I was hustling magnoleum back in the thirties. . . . Didn't think I was that old, did you now? Well-preserved, hey? the old magnoooooo-llllleeeeeuuumm sales, as the jungle bunnies used to call it.

That was a small-time thing, sure, but it had more class than this. Fake linoleum. Every spear-chucker wanted it. Paid through their ass for it. Stuff lasted about two weeks. . . ."

Phantom is off laughing again.

"Wonderful," he says. "That's exactly how long the Feldstar lasts. Two weeks to the minute. Then pop, the hands come off, the little calendar starts running backward and the watchband turns green."

"Brothers," says Howard, getting up from his seat. He comes behind us and puts his big arms around our shoulders.

"You boys are exact replicas of myself at your age. Really. Two cocky punks think you got the world by the balls. I like it. I like it fine. Don't you like it, Alice?"

"I like it," she says. "I like it fine."

Howard darts toward her, grabs her arm and twists it behind her back.

"Did I notice a trace . . . a mere trace of witchery in your voice? Oh, tell me that I didn't, dear Alice. Do not confirm my worst suspicions, thereby forcing me to give these fine plucky rascals your deeply tanned arm as a souvenir."

"You're hurting me," she says.

"Let her alone," says Phantom, slapping Howard's big shoulders. "What does she know?"

"Correct," says Howard. "A woman. Her function in the world is threefold. Dinner cooker. Childbearer. Fuck tool. Outside of those three laudable but brainless capacities, she is like a small bird lost in a den of lions."

"Hey, you are pretty heavy with words," says Phantom. "You some kind of writer?"

"Ah, the arts. The arts," says Howard, gesturing expansively. "You are acquainted with them? Not only a small-time hustler, but an artist as well? I see, I see. Rimbaud. And Baudelaire. Living for the moment. Trying desperately to transcend the

163

petty-bourgeois environments from which you both undoubtedly sprang by reveling in the exotic, the criminal. Why, you two are heroes of your age. Did you hear that, Alice? I said that these two . . ."

"I heard you, Howard," she says.

Phantom is transfixed. I am not. If I were only a little stronger (my back is hurting like mad—it's been that way ever since the Taco), I would leap at this fat bigmouth and gut him like a lion guts his prey. I shouldn't have thought that, used those words, that metaphor. It is exactly like one that Howard would use. Oh, my God, is this my next horror? To be a walking, talking verbal pyrotechnician with a fat head and a stone cold heart? I am sick. Warren is already turning, turning to a small, scale-model Howard in my brain. I won't do it. I won't look.

"Well, then," says Howard, holding his drink up in a toast, "if destiny has proclaimed that we four should spend the night together, then perhaps you two phantoms of the night can show us some new and forbidden pleasure."

I nudge Phantom. He turns around, looks at me with hostile eyes. Is he being charmed by this degenerate?

"What is it, man?"

"Let's go," I say. "We still got the air-conditioners and the fake diamonds to unload. There's no future with this guy."

"Yeah, I guess so."

"Ah, they are talking it over, Alice," says Howard. "Do you hear them mumbling a silent or nearly silent judgment on us: 'Squares. Idiots. Nowhere people. Let's ditch 'em.' But, Alice, both you and I know that is mere rationalization. They will ditch us, for they know that I have seen through their little pathetic attempts at originality, their meek, bourgeois souls. They are afraid of true decadence. You and I, Alice. The real thing. They melt from our nauseating radiance."

"Oh, Howard," says Alice, "will you please shut up?"

"So you wanna come with us?" says Phantom. "All right. Let's go. I got some things for you to see that will turn you around."

"Phantom," I say. But it's no use. His long face is drawn tense, and his big yellow teeth are gleaming.

"Lead on, O two-bit Rabelais," cries Howard as we march like prisoners from the bar.

Phantom is taking Howard and Alice on a guided tour of the Greta Garbo Hotel for Boys and Girls. Our room is on the third floor, and I am feeling like someone has filled my vessels with cancer cells. Weak. Swooning. I hope to God Mal isn't up there. Her room is two doors down from ours, and the shame and disgust I now feel will be tripled if she catches Phantom and me "proving ourselves" to this creep and his forlorn (though beautiful—all the girls I meet are always beautiful, a mockery of their inner void) wife. So far on our trip, Phantom has shown Howard Crazy Joe's room with its thirteen locks. Crazy Joe is seen rarely. He is a Japanese beatnik who sits in his room taking drugs all day. He sits in his room all night too, the only difference being that he is usually coming down off the drugs then, and entertains the rest of the floor by howling and smashing furniture. Phantom knocks on his door. Crazy Joe curses in Japanese, and Howard shakes all over.

"Marvelous, marvelous," he says. "This dispels once and for all the idea that Orientals are endowed with the secrets of the peaceful soul."

Our next visit is to Little Deena's room. She is fourteen, an acid freak, and lives with Big Hal, a former Jehovah's Witness. Now he is into acid too, and they both show us their many religious books.

"You can only understand these if you are stoned, man," says Hal. He and Deena weigh about a hundred and forty pounds combined. I look at their bony bodies and know that they will soon go mad or die.

Out in the hall, Phantom and Howard are arm in arm.

"Cretins," says Howard. "Pure golden cretins. Oh, show me more, more."

We go upstairs. On the steps is a dead rat. Howard picks it up by its tail, feigns eating it and tosses it into the face of Alice. She screams, and he almost collapses with laughter.

"In here lives Jerry, the Boy Who Ruins Lives," says Phantom.

We open the door to his room. Jerry is stark naked. In front of him is a young girl with an expensive-looking leather coat. Jerry is endowed with a baby face, and his blond hair is combed perfectly. He grabs the girl's small head, and she licks his cock.

"Hey, you guys," he says, "come on in. The liberation of Sandy Keller is about to begin."

Howard starts to go in, but Phantom closes the door.

"Why settle for that?" says Phantom. "I have a much greater treat in store for you."

That was not Phantom's voice. It was Howard's. He is being taken over by Howard. I feel my own flesh being dissolved, shoved roughly out of the way, Howard's flesh moving in.

"Phantom," I say meekly, "I've got to get some air. You take these people up to the room. I'm going for a walk."

They won't let me. Phantom has one arm, Howard the other. They are marching me up to the third floor.

"No copping out, Bobby," says Phantom. "We are . . . how'd you put it, Howard?"

"We are but children of destiny. Ships passing in the night.

166

Come on, kid. You wanted to play games. Well, we're playing them."

I look at Alice. She drops her eyes.

In the room. It's colored with the posters we put up just yesterday. I remember Mal and me tacking them there, and I stared at them with wonder. Psychedelic art. It seemed like some kind of ultimate breakthrough. I felt big, strong, like a pioneer. Now I can't look at them. Cheap, phony, nothing. Howard inside me. My T-shirt disintegrating, and a blue pinstripe suit taking its place. My stomach bulging, hanging over my belt. Like Baba Looie. Like Howard.

"So, good gurus," says Howard, sitting down on our one chair, "when does the mystery begin? So far all I've seen is petty perversity. I am beginning to think you can't deliver the goods. That would be truly pathetic, beneath pity."

I am sitting against the wall. It occurs to me that Howard is crazy. Violence. He will be fast and big and maybe even pull a knife.

Phantom is pacing the room. He stops, looks at Howard and smiles. Alice is sitting at Howard's feet, like a puppy. He smiles at her, puts one giant hand on her breasts.

"We could all fuck Alice," he says, "but then I'd be supplying the entertainment. Perhaps what you two need is some form of motivation. Some capitalist incentive. I'll tell you what. If you can deliver to my satisfaction, I'll pay you one hundred dollars. Cash."

He reaches into his pocket, pulls out the wad of bills and takes two fifties from the top. His big white fingers crease them, make a snapping noise.

"So?"

I want to smash his face. But he has cut through me, reduced me to something small, without fur or covering, a longnecked chicken waiting for the ax.

167

"Fifty, huh?" says Phantom. He rubs his hands together, runs his lizard tongue around his mouth. "O.K., Howard. You wanna do something? I got just the thing."

Phantom walks over to our small drawer and opens it with a key. He reaches far back into it, looking at Howard all the time, smiling. Howard is smiling back. They are like lovers locked together, sinking to the bottom of the sea.

"Cut the lights, Bobby."

I get up and go to the door.

The room is black.

Phantom lights a candle.

"Oh, wonderful," says Howard. "What now, Maharishi, the Ouija Board?"

"You dig this effect, man?"

"Most intriguing."

"O.K. Now I got something special for you to smoke. Then I'm gonna take you on a little trip. I never shared this with nobody before."

Though I am sick, I immediately go hot with jealousy. Phantom and I are brothers. He can't get away with this. I'll call Freda and tell her. I won't play with him anymore.

"Do I detect some bitterness from your friend, Bobby?" says Howard. "It was inevitable that someone should come and depose you as the object of your hideous demonic friend's affections."

"Shut the fuck up," I say. I'll go out on the ledge and pretend to jump. Then Phantom will be sorry. I scratch my arm deep to purge weakness.

"I was in the Orient," says Phantom, sitting down cross-legged in front of Howard and Alice.

"And while you were there you learned the way to cloud men's minds."

Don't go on, Phantom, stop now. I can't look at Phantom.

He looks small, pale, ridiculous. Every word Howard speaks shatters Phantom. I could be working for the state making a nice salary. I could save up and buy season tickets to Colt games. Howard.

"Yeah, man, I was in the Orient, and this guy laid some lessons on me in guiding people on journeys. You dig it?"

Howard is quiet, but he is smiling like a serpent.

"So if you smoke this red powder here, I can take you into some places in your head, you see?"

"Dig, cool."

Alice is twisting around.

"I don't want to, Howard," she says.

He pats her head.

"Are you or are you not Mrs. Howard Zucker?"

"Oh, Howard, you know I am, it's just that . . ."

"Give me the pipe," says Howard.

Phantom finishes spreading the tin foil on the pipe and dumps a little red powder on it. Howard grabs it away from him and sticks it in Alice's mouth.

"In sickness and in health, in death do we part." He smiles.

She pulls her head away, but Howard seizes her chin.

"No, Howard," she gasps. "I don't want to."

"Smoke, bitch. Smoke the pipe."

He waves his right hand like a minstrel singer, and Phantom lights the match.

She gives in and smokes it, but is unable to hold it down long. The candle is flickering shadows all over her face. Her eyes are wide open, in panic. Howard grabs the pipe himself.

"Disgusting," he says. "The wife of Howard K. Zucker responding to the exotic like a Victorian."

Phantom relights the pipe and Howard takes a tremendous breath. Then he slides to the floor and leans back on his hands. His stomach is moving in-out, in-out. Phantom is smiling.

I move closer and watch Howard's face. It is perfectly calm, mocking. Alice has fallen straight back and is gasping. I go over to her and hold her hand.

"Oh my God," she says. "It's like . . ."

She can't say anything else. Her face is frozen.

"When's this stuff hit?" says Howard. Then he is falling straight back. He begins to swallow, gropes at the blanket. Phantom is leaning on top of him, grabbing his chin.

"Look right into my eyes," he says. "Right now, Howard."

I pick up Alice, take her into the kitchen and throw water onto her face. She is crying hysterically. I feel sick. Want to race in and grab Phantom, smash Howard. What the hell is wrong with me? We've proved our point.

"What the hell is it, Warren? What is wrong?"

"Cockledoodle dooo, cockledoodle dooo."

I look into the front room. Phantom is standing over Howard, yelling, "And what does the rooster tell the farmer each and every sunny morning?"

Howard is stooping on the floor. His fingers are wriggling claws. His eyes are bulging.

"Cockledoodle doooooooo."

"Right," says Phantom. "And now maybe the rooster is thirsty?"

Howard nods his head vigorously.

Phantom unzips his fly, pulls out his cock and pisses in his face. Howard laughs and falls down.

"What does the rooster say?" yells Phantom.

"Cockledoodle dooo. Ahhhh cockledoodle dooo."

I should have known. Phantom wasn't taken in. I should feel happiness. I'm gonna feel happiness. I run in the room, dropping Alice on the floor.

"Let me try it?" I yell.

"Sure," says Phantom.

170

"What does the rooster say?" I yell.

"Cockledoodle dooo," yells Howard. His mouth is wide open and his tongue is going in-out.

I take out my cock and piss on him. The urine runs down his face, stains his blue striped shirt. I grab his tie and yank him around in a circle.

"You sonofabitch," I yell. "You rotten sonofabitch."

"That's it, baby," yells Phantom. He is on Howard's back, and I am pulling Howard forward.

"Rooster loves the farmer," yells Phantom. "Give him a ride, anytime. Yeah."

Alice is up now. She looks at us, screams and then starts laughing.

"Let me ride him," she yells. "Let me."

She leaps on Howard's back and I yank him forward. He begins to scream. I am having fun. I am getting even. The sonofabitch can't get away with this shit, can't tell us the truth about ourselves. We'll show the sonofabitch. Going round and round in circles, the candlelight flickering amoebas all over the wall, and the screams over and over and over, "Cockledoodle dooooooo."

Then there is a knock at the door. Perfect. Perfect. I know who it is.

"Come in, Mal," I yell.

She walks in the door, stares at us and then closes it.

Phantom jumps off Howard and runs after her. I let go of the tie and sink down on the floor. Alice is crying again, holding her hands over her face.

"He'll kill me," she says. "When he wakes up from this, he'll kill me."

I look at her. There's nothing to do. I can hear Phantom yelling at Mal out in the hall, explaining the whole scene. Howard is rolling over on his back now, rubbing his face. I

171

reach over, grab his arm and pull him up. He nearly crushes me. Mal and Phantom come back in the room.

"Get him a cab," I say.

"Fuck him, throw him out in the street. Her too, that sniveling bitch."

Phantom reaches down on the chair and grabs the two fifties.

"Get him a cab," I say. "He did me a favor."

I can't look at Mal. My hands are shaking again.

"I'll call one," says Mal.

"What do you mean, he did you a favor?" says Phantom.

"Nothing, just being melodramatic."

Phantom looks at me, through me.

"Told you where you were at, did he?"

"Just help me get him downstairs."

Phantom nods his head. This is the end of something. He grabs Howard under his sweating arm and we drag him toward the door. All the way down the steps Howard is laughing and mumbling to himself, "What does the rooster say? 'Cockle-doodle doooooooo.' "

XXX.
Our Hero Has Love and Lessons on the Beach

Mal and I are walking on the beach, holding hands, watching and listening to the ocean. Even Warren is silent. It should be an ideal scene, and I want very much to say something tender and romantic. But that isn't possible. The movies screwed us up. We smoked a lot of hash and went to see a double feature at a drive-in. One of the pictures was about a "contemporary love affair" and featured many shots of young lovers strolling down beaches. Now I know that if I speak softly it will seem like I am parroting the movie. But that isn't the real problem. The real problem is that I am afraid to speak softly. I am afraid of Mal. She knows more than I do. She has control, where I am still steaming, running like a man with a bag over my head, from one thing to the next. We keep walking, bare feet dragging through the sand. But I am not relaxed.

"I love the ocean," she says. "It's . . ."

"What?"

"I don't want to say it. You and Phantom would think I'm simpleminded."

Me and Kirk. Me and Walter. Me and Phantom. I want to strangle.

"Say it, will you? I want to hear it. God knows, I can't talk."

Now Mal stops. She puts her arms around me.

"That's the first honest thing you have ever said."

I nod my head, throw away my cigarette.

I look at my feet. The toes are pointed in like Randy's. I am a rag doll made of parts of my friends.

Mal holds both my hands and looks into my eyes.

"You should come with me to Big Sur," she says.

"Yeah?"

"Yeah." Her voice is gruff, like my own.

"Are you mocking me, madam?"

"No. It's just . . . well, why do you always come off like the Phantom, or like some Zachary Scott desperado from an old movie? You're cheating yourself."

I sit down and light another cigarette. The breeze is blowing through me. Transparent.

"You know you don't have to," she says, "not with me. If you'll pardon the cliché, I know you're good; and you don't need games."

I shrug my shoulders. I didn't want to.

"Let me tell you about Big Sur, Bobby. You really ought to go there. There's a farm there, a commune, called Taurus. It's run by my friends, Gary Biffel and some others."

And I sit there and listen to her, watch her hands moving back and forth and her eyes lighting up, reflecting the waves as they slosh in over the beach. Another Susan? Another Lily? No . . .

"You see," she says, "you can't get anywhere unless you stop

174

and slow down. Adventures, dreams, it's all intoxicating, but it's all illusions. The Head . . ."

"Wait a minute," I say. "You aren't going to start quoting the Head to me, are you? I already read his shit in the papers. Talk about illusions . . . that guy is throwing out stone lies."

"How do you know?" she says. "All you're doing is racing about. Gary Biffel—the guy I was just telling you about—well, he is the Head, and he's about the most enlightened person I've ever met."

So we are sitting still, very still now, and Mal is telling me how the Head and his friends have learned to live together and share things, which enables them to beat the private-property hang-up, and how personal identity is just an illusion anyway, because you are nothing more than your relationships with the world. And though I have heard all this before, now, with the moonlight glancing off Mal's golden bracelets and her black hair twisting around her neck, somehow it all makes perfect sense.

"You see, Bobby, if you think of yourself as an individual, separate and unique from others, and then suddenly you realize that this isn't so, it can throw you into a kind of panic. I mean, you start realizing that you are picking up bits and snatches from everyone else, and you can't hear your own voice at all. But what you have to realize is that you can never do anything about it unless you give up the entire idea of individualism. It's an illusion."

"I see," I say. And I do see. Perfect. Her skin, her almond eyes, her black hair. I hold her hand tightly and pull her closer to me.

"You have to go somewhere, Bobby, where people will let you be yourself, where there is a kind of peace, and an atmosphere of trust and friendliness. Someplace where you don't have to be on stage all the time . . ."

175

"Yes," I say, breathless. The moon and the stars and this incredible girl who knows what she is talking about.

"And when you stay there for a while, you'll find yourself realizing, hearing your own voice, but you'll realize it's the common voice of all the other people, and that fact won't bother you at all. Do you understand?"

"Yes." And I am pulling her close and kissing her forehead. Boy, would I like to jam my cock up her ass. It's terrific. I'll kill myself if I think that way again, I swear it.

"You just take acid out in the woods, or even like this, down on the beach, and you understand, the way the old Romantic poets understood, about nature and our relationship to it."

Not just her ass, but my cock whammmmo! tight in her mouth. I mean, it looks like her mouth has been made expressly for my cock. How can I think shit like this? Am I an animal?

"And, Bobby . . . ohh . . . I mean, once you . . . ohh . . . once you learn about the community thing you'll realize how silly, how ridiculous . . . wait a minute . . . the whole idea of a unique personality is anyway."

If I had two cocks I could have one in her mouth and another up her ass. If I had three cocks . . . What if arms were cocks or could be transformed into cocks at any moment? Say you reached a certain level of horniness, and your arms just whoof! turned into cocks. If I can get these pants off with my teeth . . .

And she is throbbing now, moving her ass up in the air, and my mouth is on her thigh, and my tongue licking her beautiful juicy cunt, and the ocean is sloshing in, and she is still talking:

"And finally . . . ohhhhuhhh . . . once you have gotten to your deepest self and into the group's deepest self, oh my goddddd . . . you will . . . see—oh Jesus, Bobby, eat me . . . that the whole thing . . . that's it, come up here, I

176

want to kiss you, put it in me . . . that the whole thing is just like a big global village, and oh Christ I love your cock . . . we all come from the same godhead . . . love your fucking cock . . ."

And we are pounding away, and the moon is coming down, and the surf is roaring in, boomalay boomalay boomalay boom, and now just when I am ready to really turn it on, just as she is moaning and her wonderful mystical ass is three feet off the sand, I start thinking of those rotten fucking movies we saw tonight, and all the rotten fucking movies with this amazing, beautiful scene in them, and I am Burt Lancaster, and she is Deborah Kerr, and there it goes, the surf, and the moon and the crabs, and my cock is melting melting melting like an icicle left out in the sun.

"Ah fuck," I say, throwing sand into the air.

"It's all right," she says, holding the two dried prunes under my limp dick.

"Soon we go to Taurus, and it will be all right."

XXXI.
In Which the Narrator Suffers from a Bad Dream

I wake up in the middle of the night. The Taco is above me.
The worker's gold watch is gleaming and his mouth is drooling
spittle. I am not awake. This is a dream. I am awake. I can see
him lifting the Taco onto his own back. I am inside his skin.
Phantom is across our single room. Mal's room is three doors
down. We are living in a huge, broken-down hotel in the
Japanese sector of San Francisco. Yesterday, Phantom and I
went into Japanese homes not three blocks from where we
live. We sold them Air King air-conditioners for seventeen
dollars apiece. The Air King consists of a metal box with three
shiny dials on it. The dials are from old radios. I am inside
the worker's skin, and he is holding the Taco above his head.
I am directly beneath the Taco. I am praying that he will not
choose to drop it on me. I open my mouth to plead, but
suddenly I see the watch. Two weeks are almost up. The watch

is making buzzing noises. The worker's teeth are clenched. The Taco is dripping hot sauce. Every drop singes my skin, leaving black marks. I want to scream, but when I open my mouth, all that comes out is a stream of old Colt tickets. The Taco is bursting, showering. Phantom is right behind the worker. In his hands are Zircons. He is telling this Japanese store owner that these are real diamonds which he heisted, and the cops are on his trail. He will leave these diamonds with the Japanese store owner because he knows that Orientals have a tradition of personal honesty and a complete disdain for material wealth. The Japanese store owner looks at the Zircons and then at Phantom's face. He says he will be glad to keep the diamonds for Phantom until such time as Phantom deems it safe enough to return from his mountain hideout to pick the jewels up. Phantom says he completely trusts the Japanese store owner, but asks him, as a token of good faith, to please give him a small retainer. The Japanese store owner's eyes are the eyes of the workman are the eyes of Baba Looie are the eyes of myself as I cringe and plead that the workman not drop the Taco on my head. I have never learned to tread meat. The watch is smoking on the workman's hairy wrist, and I know that begging is useless. Phantom stop. Japanese store owner stop. The face of Japanese mother stop. All of them the same eyes. All of them the same smell. Every pore emitting greed gases, and I am in an old hotel, not awake, not asleep. The Air King consists of a metal box, radio dials. Inside is a stainless steel pan filled with three inches of water. Above and behind it is a little electric fan. The Japanese mother is shelling out seventeen dollars to Phantom and me, while her kids sweat in the background. She plugs it in, complains that it doesn't seem cool enough. We tell her that it takes an hour to warm up. She smiles. Her children surround her and wait for great gusts of kamikaze winds. We thank her and bow ceremoniously.

I am in a hotel. This is a dream from which there is no waking, no way to wake up. . . .

"Don't drop it," I yell. "Don't drop it."

"Hey, hey, hey, what the hell?"

Mal is above me, and Phantom. I am trembling now for real, and my eyes are open. I can't remember where I am.

"Bummer," says Phantom, slapping my face.

Mal is kneeling on the floor in front of me.

"What's wrong, Bobby?" she is saying. "Hey, it's O.K."

I open my eyes. I don't remember where I am. I can't think of my name. The reels are running in the back of my head again.

"Jesus," I say, hugging her. Then I get embarrassed. Is this Mother Freda compensation?

"I can't take no more hustles," I say to Phantom. "There is no way."

He nods his head. From downstairs I can hear the Jefferson Airplane. Yeah, I am living in the Greta Garbo Hotel for Boys and Girls. Speed freaks downstairs. A little guy named Red who shoots Methedrine all day and talks endlessly about white lights.

"I, ah, yeah, I'm all right."

They nod, smile, move away from me. Mal opens the window and I look out across the skyline at the Bay Bridge.

"Yeah," says Phantom, "I have had enough of this criminal bag myself. You have to hang around with too many low-lifes. Ugh . . . that Howard Zucker. What a disgusting cat. I'm going to make it to Berkeley tomorrow."

The mention of Howard Zucker makes my skin melt. I feel as though my body is turning to water. I am afraid to talk because my voice is disappearing. I don't want to hear myself doing Phantom.

"Wait, Phantom. Before you go to Berkeley, let's take acid

together. I think it would be like starting all over. You know?"

Phantom smiles at Mal. There is no trace of bitterness and, what's more, I recognize the smile. It's my own.

"O.K.," he says. "All right, my brothers. Tomorrow."

Then he smiles at me.

"You stay here with this creep awhile," he says. "I got to go take back a few of those old Feldstars."

When he leaves, Mal walks toward my bed.

"He's really all right, you know?" she says.

Then she drops off her dress and eases into bed.

XXXII.
A Buffalo with Kissable Lips

The acid comes on like an elevator which is going twenty times as fast as the speed of light and you know it's going to go right through the roof, you know that when it does you will be blown to hell, and there is a moment, as we stand in front of the buffalo cages across from the polo fields in Golden Gate Park, that you are going to give way to panic, to no control, but suddenly you have gone through that roof, and yes, it was only a paper roof anyway, and you are with your friends, your closest friends in the world, Mal and Phantom, and you are certain, certain that there has never before been a beauty to equal this, never.

"So, dig those buffaloes," says Phantom.

And yes, I am standing here behind the wire mesh, my nose pressed up to it actually, and I am rushing, rushing with a color kind of pleasure that is incredible blue, funny, profound, sad and wide, all at once and I am watching this great, hairy monster with impossibly little pinny legs standing in a field.

"Isn't it beautiful?" says Mal.

"Yeah, beautiful," says Phantom. His mouth is hanging open, Phantom's that is, and his skin is changing right here in front of me, folks, see the Phantom with the changing skin, and I shut my eyes and am reminded of the skin of someone else, so long ago, someone whose skin changed without acid, and then I remember. Yes, it was the skin of Johnny D., who was a disk jockey in Baltimore, an incredible disk jockey who had an incredible contest called Miss Kissable Lips, which Freda entered when I was so small I did not know what was happening; but I saw Freda spend one entire afternoon blotting her lips on a piece of tagboard to send to Johnny D.

And then we were in the studio auditorium, and Johnny D. had golden bleacho hair, and he was presenting all the finalists for the Miss Kissable Lips contest.

"Look, there's the young buffalo."

I stare out of my 1958 dream world and in front of me is a little buffalo, right in front of me, how can this be?

I place my hand through the mesh, not afraid that this animal will take it off, not afraid of anything, but why does Phantom's skin, all red and blotchy, remind me of Johnny D., for now I know that Johnny D. had perfect baby-pink skin, like all those 1950s announcers. Then I see what it is. Phantom's skin reminds me of Johnny D.'s dark 1950s soul. That is it, the soul of the 1950s and early '60s. This is what I am seeing, hearing, total re-creation, when I shut my eyes and see Mother Freda turning turning around on this high, velvet-covered pedestal with the name Red Night Shoes on it.

"Look at their eyes," says Mal.

And I am out of that scene and staring into the bloodshot,

yellow-phlegm eyes of the American bison. I know that Mal wants the animal to be something mystical for me, and I strain to see it her way.

"The Indians worshiped this animal," says Phantom.

All our noses pressed to the wire, mine, Phantom's and Mal's, and the buffalo is looking like some great, grotesque clown to me, with that huge, hulking, hairy body and those little weeny legs, and now, oh now, he is standing up on those legs, and Johnny D. is asking all the judges, all dapper men in gray 1950s pin-stripe suits with pictures of Eisenhower smiling moronic from the soaked golf courses of their 1950s hearts, and Freda is still twirling, what a weird revelation to have on acid, but I know I can turn it off, soak myself into the sounds of the park, the grass so green it looks like pea soup pictures in *Family Circle* magazine ads, I know I can leave 1950 but there is some secret there for me, some horror that I must uncover, buffalo come back into view, still standing on those little pin legs, and now Freda still turning turning around, dressed in a long, one-piece bathing suit made of terry cloth, and her stomach sticking out so far I am afraid she will suffer from permanent skin stretch, and have to fold the skin over and pretend it's her apron when she goes off to Methodist Women's League.

"Oh, it's so mystical."

And I am back with the buffalo, which is standing on those pin legs, and beginning to ooze out a huge, liquid shit, so brown that it looks like soft chocolate ice cream found in every drive-in all over the U.S.A. But what is flipping me most is the reaction of both Mal and Phantom. They are in a mystical ecstasy about this.

Mal: "Oh God, look at it. It's overpowering."

Phantom: "Stone beautiful."

Then I realize that they are lying. They must be lying. Maybe Mal thinks it's beautiful and Phantom is agreeing with her because he knows he has hurt her before. Or maybe not. Maybe it is beautiful. Maybe I cannot see. And I stick my face closer to the fence and watch the buffalo's little paws shaking as the goo rushes from his asshole onto the greenest grass under the stars, and I am more aware of the fence, its coldness, which seems more of a miracle to me than buffalo shitting. But I want to share this with them. God, I want it. Absurd, senseless, ridiculous, but I want to share this buffalo shit with them so bad, as bad as Freda wanted Johnny D. to make her Miss Kissable Lips, and she went around and around on that pedestal her stomach gonna burst through her skin, leaving long lines of entrails, and God I want to share it with them, God I love them, these my friends, and I am laughing at the buffalo, crying for Mother Freda's kissable lips, and all around us are the fog and crickets, all over the park.

XXXIII.
Moving Down the Coast with Kevin Balso

Standing at the entrance to the freeway, Mal with her thumb stuck in the air, and we are singing "Break On Through": We have not even gotten through the first chorus when a car stops for us, and in a flash we are sailing over the curvy highway at seventy miles an hour. The driver is a fat, thirtyish man named Kevin Balso. He sells Hotpoint ranges, "the kind you see on all them TV game shows, you know?"

"Sure," says Mal, lighting a joint.

"What are you doing?" I whisper to her. "You can't smoke in this dude's car."

But she only smiles and hands it to me. The man is so busy wiping the sweat off his round, deep-ridged forehead that he hasn't noticed what's going down. But I am certain he will, and then we'll be thrown out of the car. Resigning myself to a short ride, I take a deep drag off the joint, and look at the man's head. He has interesting hair, which looks like little

186

steps on the way up to heaven. I imagine the hair latching onto a star. The man will be walking into his house and his wife will throw her hands up to her face, certain that she has married a god.

"Your hair, Kevin. It's got stars. . . ."

But he will not hear what she is saying or care, for in his hands is the latest in Hotpoint All Electric Ranges, cooks the food for you, sticks it in your mouth and wipes your ass right after you take a crap.

"I'm from Saint Louis myself," the man says, turning on a station which is playing a song which is a sequel to "Ode to Billy Joe." It's about a girl who really knows why Billy Joe jumped off the bridge, and of course Kevin Balso cannot tell the songs apart.

"That's a great song," he says, humming along off key.

"Too much," says Mal. I look at her and realize that she likes Kevin Balso and his simple, moronic happiness. Come to think of it, I like him too. After all, he did pick us up, and he *is* singing, and the car is going along eighty-five, and the telephone poles are sailing by like broomsticks from *The Sorcerer's Apprentice*, so what the hell?

"I am from Saint Louis originally," he says, wiping his forehead off again, puffing smoke from his nostrils.

I tell him that I was recently there. This excites him very much, and he asks me if I saw the new stadium.

"It goes around on tracks," he says.

I take several more puffs from the joint and try to figure out what he is telling me. I look at Mal. Her eyes have gotten very sleepy and she is smiling at our host.

"Sir," she says, "do you mean to say that the stadium goes around on tracks while the team is playing?"

"That sounds like fun," I say.

"No," says Kevin Balso, laughing. "I mean . . ."

But Mal is onto her own fantasy.

"Can't you see it, Mr. Balso?" she says. "Someone kicking a field goal with three minutes to play, and his team down by two points, and the ball is sailing right and true, when suddenly, the whole thing goes around on tracks, and the ball continues on its flight, but straight through the other team's crossbar, so without knowing it, you who kicked the ball have unwittingly aided and abetted the opposing team in scoring a crucial three-point play which spells destruction for your side."

"Gee," says Kevin Balso, biting his lower lip.

As I lie back and stare at the road, I see a wincry advertisement.

SAN MATEO WINE—STOP AND SAMPLE OUR LUSCIOUS PRODUCT

"Hey," I say. "Look at that."

"I will tell you one thing," says Kevin Balso, lifting his eighth glass of Hawaiian Delight wine. "This would sure make a great story to tell old Fred Carr back at the Hotpoint office."

Mal takes his hands and asks him why it *would* make a good story, and Kevin rubs his cheek against her fingers and stares out the wire-covered windows with a sad expression on his face.

"I can't tell anyone about this," he says. "It's not good business to pick people up in the first place, and if they knew I was out getting lushed with some hippies . . ."

He shakes his head at the mere thought of it.

Then Mal hands him another glass. I am sticking to Red Mountain wine myself. It's cheap and what we are used to drinking.

"What the hell," says Kevin suddenly. "I don't know what I'm gonna do."

His eyes are wild and terrified.

"What do you mean?"

"I mean this," he says, slamming the glass down on the oak table. "I mean I am thirty-four years old and I am making ten thousand a year, and I want to know what the hell I'm going to do."

Several tourists are looking at us now. Kevin's eyes are popping, and his Adam's apple is jumping up and down like the guy who used to be in the old "Behind the Eight Ball" comedies.

"I mean what the hell is the use of this crap? I know the electric range business like I know the back of my hand, but what the hell is the use?"

Mal is holding his hand and I am staring at him completely whacked out and all of a sudden I am seeing Glenn there in front of me. This is a young Glenn, and then I understand that there is something very wrong here, not only with Glenn, don't you see, but very wrong with all of it, that every one of us is facing this thing, all of us will have the "electric range despair," and this flash makes me shudder, brings me down with a terrible crash.

But Mal is amazing. She is leading Kevin Balso, who is actually weeping now, weeping as we walk past a little old lady in a Swiss Winemaker's Costume with genuine imitation wood shoes on, and too much rouge so she looks like a wooden doll, and Mal is saying in this sweet, controlled and loving voice, "It's all right, Kevin. It's all right. We love you. We really do love you."

And then we are out in the parking lot, sitting in the front seat of his car, and Kevin Balso has his head on the back of the front seat, and Mal is rubbing her hands through his hair, and chanting to him over and over, "It's really all right, Kevin. You're gonna make it."

Then Kevin does a strange thing. As quickly as he broke down, he has himself back together.

"Hey," he says, his eyes still dripping with tears. "That stuff you were saying about the tracks. That was pretty funny. You two are all right."

Mal is still rubbing his head, and I am getting nervous. I have seen this before, and am waiting for him to start feeling embarrassed about his crackup. When that happens, the hostility begins.

But because of Mal it doesn't happen. Because she is staring directly into him, and rubbing his head, and she is lighting up a joint and telling him in the smoothest voice in the world to take deep breaths and hold it as long as he can, and incredibly he is saying "O.K., O.K., I trust you. I like you, Mal."

Then, right here on the parking lot of the San Mateo Winery, where there are whole families with stone gray American faces, a Hotpoint salesman is taking deep breaths and hugging Mal. Then I am in the middle of them both somehow, a joint stuck in my mouth, and the sun is burning, the cars whizzing by steaming, speeding steel, and we are hugging each other, and laughing, and somewhere out of all this sweat and flesh comes a new, hysterical voice saying, "Oh yeah, I see, it goes around on tracks."

XXXIV.
At Taurus—In Which I Realize Some Laws of the Universe

Mal shades her eyes with her hand and stares down the long green slopes to the Pacific Ocean.

"It may have gone commercial like everyone says, Bobby, but it's still beautiful here."

I smile at her and sit down on the bumper of the Head's pickup truck. He is inside the Coastline Restaurant and I am worried. The reason I am worried is the big sign on the front of the place:

A HIPPIE IS JUST A RAT WHO IS AFRAID TO JOIN THE RACE

"Do you suppose Head'll have any trouble?"

She comes back and pats me patronizingly on the arm.

"Some people might. If you or one of the other people from the farm came here, it would be very shaky; but with Head . . . well, it's different. I know what you think about vibes and

191

all that . . . I mean, you agree with the Phantom, but . . well, you've met Head now. Can't you see what I mean?"

I shrug my shoulders, but there is no use pretending. Head is a highly impressive person; and since the Kevin Balso incident on the way down here, I have become very excited. The old feelings again. Like the Taco maybe, but cleaner, and certainly not as hot. Warren is whispering to me, that impudent fruit, that Head's muttonchops, brown-blond hair, white robes knitted by South American Indians, and red bellbottoms are pure decadence; but I see no reason to hang a man for looking his best. Still, it is not the visual appeal of Head that has knocked me out. It is the effortless way he makes you feel at home, the undeniable physical grace in his every movement, the low, almost shy tone of voice he uses, as if the wisdom he has learned while traveling in India must not be contaminated by boasting or ego games.

"Head will feel mystical in heaven after this red-necked tavern owner puts a dumdum in his belly," hisses Warren.

"Buzz off," I say.

No sooner have we made that banal exchange than Head comes out of the doorway with a package of ice. The bartender is patting him on the back and Head is handing him something. I watch him walk toward us. He sees me and waves. Mal turns to me, smiling.

"Head is too much," I say.

I feel a great warmth and imagine myself helping Kevin Balsos everywhere. If only Head will give up his secrets. Mal hands me a joint and we watch Head walk like a cat. Behind him is a Ford with a man and a woman inside. They are not watching Head (they probably don't even know him), but are staring at something out the passenger's window. I look up and see a sea gull sailing over the clouds. In his beak is a live, flapping fish. Head turns to look also. So does the driver of the car. I am horrified. The car is going right into Head's path, and I am the only one who knows what is going to happen. Head will lie crushed in ice. But for some reason (what?), I cannot yell. And as I watch them point their brown fingers out the window at the gull, I realize why people in Cleveland stood around the body. They were participating in the only way they knew how, and that is to watch. What confused them (and now Head is close to death, and now the wife is smiling big white smiles with her idiot teeth) is what is confusing me. That is, this play they (and not I) were watching was not surrounded by a frame. They knew somehow that this play was *different* from the plays they watched every night in their comfortable chairs, but they were not certain *how* it was different. I am certain that they sang with the Phantom because it was their way of supplying theme music to the play. And so, as Head steps along unknowingly, and as the husband's mouth opens and his eyes see Head, I hum a little tune and put my hands around my eyes, in the shape of a box, and it works. It works perfectly. This is television and I am the director.

But, apparently, there is a part of me that does not believe that this is only a play, and I find myself screaming "Look out, Head," which he does. The car, then, is the only thing left in the play; and it slams into the rear of a blue Sprite. But I am no longer interested in the drama, for I am thinking that never before the last month have I been involved in a car wreck, but suddenly I am involved in three of them. I think of this as some kind of cosmic coincidence, for all the wrecks have shown me something about the world. This insight brings about a chemical change in my body, and I begin to feel as though I have the energy of Superman. Still standing very still, I know that I am giving off electric impulses to Head, and that he is receiving them, and that somehow, through dumb luck,

I have hit upon a magical law of the Universe, and that is: *Everything happens to you, and you have no way of stopping it, but if you just go with it, you will see that you controlled it all along, and if you didn't control it, then what difference does it make?*

I reach into my pocket, pull out a stubby pencil and write these thoughts down on a crushed-up match pack which features an advertisement from George Pectoralis. The ad shows a skinny runt of a kid with a cowlick and a look of deep malaise on his face. Then there is a totally different kid standing next to him, who I am supposed to believe is the same kid after reading and doing the exercises in a book called *Big Body*. This phrase strikes me like one of the hammers on the old Anacin commercials. For it brings to mind something which I had nearly forgotten, and which makes instant sense if examined under my newly found Principle of the Universe. What I remember is my father's fascination with weights. I see him down our dark cellar, sitting on his red vinyl weight lifter's bench, his neck muscles bulging as he tries to do curls with black steel dumbbells. I am sitting on the cellar steps and he is telling me that the body does not take care of itself, and that a man must do these exercises if he does not want to suffer from hanging stomach and flabby, puffed-up arms. I watch him, sitting there with his knobby knees shivering beneath the swinging bare bulb, and I watch the shadows on the gray cement and my father's nose getting redder and redder, and I ask him quite innocently if he is Rudolph the Red-Nosed Reindeer. My father does not take this lightly. He pulls me down into the dungeon with him and makes me try to lift the weights, but I cannot. I ask him if I can go upstairs, but he is furious and says, "C'mon, smart guy, lemme see if you can put your money where your mouth is." And I strain and strain, using two hands, but it is no use. I cannot budge it from the floor. I try to run away but he is in front of me, laughing a Dracula laugh, and pointing back down at the weights. When I refuse, he picks me up and lays me on the bench. Then he takes the big barbell and lays it across my neck. When I try to lift up, I see the words "York Barbell Company" on the steel. I curse and cry, but he has gone upstairs to the bathroom, and I am forced to lie on the cold plastic bench until Freda gets home from Social Club.

And as all these images come back to me, I understand that my father never made it because he did not understand the simplest premise of things. He thought he could wrench himself free of his mortality through weights, through action, but this is not so. *It is all happening to us and we must go with it.* The thought strikes me as pure revelation and I am amazed that it has taken me so long to realize it. I do not realize that I have been laughing at these same ideas when they were written up in the papers by Head. I do not realize that I have been fighting everything that has been thrown my way since I was old enough to think. All I can feel is the illumination I am getting, the energy and electric impulse I am getting, and I am flattened by the simplicity of it, the wonder of the simplicity. And then, whap! comes another revelation, and that is about Head. He has been sent to me with an offering. Just as the Stumps, and the Phantom, and the Aces (who are all thrown into relief like cardboard cutouts in my children's books, who are towering figures, prophets who have helped me reach this undeniable moment of truth) were sent to me. I race over and help Head pick up the spilled ice. It runs through my hands but I pay no attention to it. I must aid my Teacher.

"The ice . . ." I say.

"Do not worry," he says to me, stroking his mustache and looking disinterestedly at the mothers and the babies who are shaking their heads at their ripped-up fenders.

195

"Ice is easy to come by," he says, "but life isn't. I should have known they were behind me. It reveals a failure in my concentration."

Yes, I think. Your mind must have been somewhere else. Your mind must have been on the icy planet Jupiter. You were high atop some craggy, glacial peak. You were holding your hands high above your head, and you were gazing into the infinite stars and knowing exactly what they knew, and you were in such a blissful state that no mother and her pudgy, sticky-fingered kid could ever reach you. And if they had hit you, it would have made no difference, because . . . because in the state of mind you were in, the metal of the car would have passed right through you, and it was lucky for those mothers that they did not hit you because it would have been they who suffered the shock, not you. The experience would have fractured them, for they would have known, finally known, that they had lived a lie for all these years, that spiritually they were deep within the bottom of a huge canal, while all along there were other people (only a few) who were swimming in the vast, psychedelic ocean, free, free of all the hangups and ego games, and keeping up with the Joneses, and Cougars, and barbecue pits, and Little League. (And now suddenly I remember that I never made the Little League team, that every time I went out for the Waverly Indians I would become fractured by fear and pain, and after the first practice they would stick me way out in right field where no one ever hit the ball. . . . I see myself out there, knowing they are going to have a "cut" today, and I must do well, I have to make the team, *Jesus, what if I don't, what if I can't play, and the ball is hit to me, I see it coming on a slice, in the sun, and I am digging digging for it knowing that I am going to drop it, knowing that the fat cigar-smoking manager who works at a steel plant and hates me because I am the wise guy*

196

on the team will put his arm around me and say with a patronizing voice, "son, only so many can make the squad, and it's a hell of a thing to hafta tell you, but . . .") But nothing, nothing, for now I know why I dropped the ball, and understand that I did what I really wanted to do, and that is not play at all, not play the game, not dress in the hot flannel suit and play on the crabgrass field, that I wanted to do nothing, only I didn't know that I wanted to do nothing, which is why I got so fucked up. Yes, Head, but you do know, I can see it in your eyes, feel it on the little curled ends of your mustache, and I too know now, so let's go back to Taurus and begin working on what's really real.

And now we are speeding along, and I am feeling a confidence and a realness that have never before existed. Head has opened up a bit and is telling me about his past, how he is from Montana, and how his father is *still* in Montana drinking himself to death, but now that he is onto Krishna Consciousness he doesn't give a good shit about that.

"I really wanna learn it," I say.

"Perhaps you will," he says, "but it takes time."

And I nod and laugh to myself because if there's one thing I got it's time, for what is time but some manmade concept to induce people to get to work on *time*. And who is going to work, who is going to be trapped by time, live inside time's barren yard, when there are moonlight and stars and the warmth of the sun?

I sit on an Indian rug in the center of the living room and I meet so many beautiful people that I cannot remember their names, and do not care if I do, for one of them has hit me with an important idea. Names do not matter; what matters is essence. If I am called Bob or Doggie, there is no difference. I hear the words, as if they come barreling down a long tunnel, a fast freight that is running straight into my brain and heart.

"Yeah, I see," I say, astonished. For this bit of information is in exact correspondence with my insight out on the parking lot, the insight of everything happening. After smoking five joints of Acapulco Gold and listening silently (for there is sound even in silence, as Head and Mal have told me) to the music of the Grateful Dead, I tell (in a low, reverent voice, the voice of a man who has been humbled beneath the importance of the Ultimate) the gathering of my amazing car wreck experiences.

"And what do you get from that, man?" says Head, as he leans on his lacy elbows, smoking another joint.

I stare at Mal, afraid to speak. She smiles and speaks for me:

"You were going to say that you felt the Universe is trying to tell you something."

I am dumbfounded.

"Yes," I say, "that is exactly what I had in mind. The universe . . . beautiful."

This is the first time I have ever used the word "beautiful" without feeling self-conscious. I suddenly see that these people are my brothers. They are on the same path as myself. Head hands me amphetamine and a needle, and I do not hesitate in letting Mal tie me up. I smile as she tightens her Navajo headband around my bulging veins. When the needle goes into my arm, I do not faint, but enjoy the blood as it is being drawn back into the syringe. And immediately the word "enjoy" takes on a new connotation.

"We are here to enjoy this planet," I say, as my mind is carried out of my body, two hundred miles a second. The heart beating beneath my skin, fast, faster (only the briefest of thoughts about heart attacks, and I laugh it off).

"Beautiful," says someone.

"Wow," says someone else.

And I understand (now) that these words are codes to those of us who know their secret meanings. And I am struck with wonder that all this is rushing into me, all this secret knowledge that is as plain as the nose on any grandmother's face. This knowledge which can free the *whole world* and make everything simple and beautiful, and now Mal shows me a flower, and puts it behind my ear, and whispers to me that she thinks I am beautiful, that we are all beautiful.

"Yeah," I say. "Yeah, beautiful. We are all beautiful and . . ."

But Head interrupts me with a serious look. He stands above me, forty feet tall.

"You are going to learn some more secrets very soon," he says. "Tonight our brothers are coming for the chanting."

"Grooooooooooooooooooooovy," says a small blond girl with hair all over her legs, and the sound of the words trails out like music or like a stream of beautiful white smoke which is thick in front of your eyes, and then slowly, slowly, blows into the air and back into the void from which it came.

It is the night of the meeting, we are waiting in the farm-house attic, Head has lent me his clothes to wear. I have on black felt pants, and a flower-stained shirt, and authentic Mexican boots. I hope that the sweat pouring off my body does not smell these wonderful garments up. I picture Head flying into a rage, telling me that every vision I have had is canceled out by my foul body odor. It occurs to me that this is a paranoid thought, which I should not be having, for how can I have paranoid thoughts when there is no me. (This is an important concept in Krishna Consciousness, as I understand it. Since you and the Universe are the same thing, it is impossible to have any negative thoughts, for all is perfect in the cycle, and that includes even terrible things like bad thoughts. When Head told me this I recognized it as circular logic, and this circular aspect of it fits in with the whole, for everything in a circle comes back to everything else and all is one.) In spite of that fact, I must admit to a certain amount of trepidation. I am sweating all over, and my hair is greasy, and my heart keeps skipping beats, which is no fun at all. Also, the room has changed. I don't mean that one of the Taurus commune girls pranced in and exercised her feminine touch on the furniture, for in this tribe, a Krishna tribe, there is no real difference between men and women; therefore, a woman would not have these feminine instincts. What I do mean is the shadows from the candle which looked so warm and inviting just a few hours ago now seem ominous and terrifying. And the Gothic faces carved on the feet of Head's antique chair, which he bought so cheap up in San Francisco on quaint old McAllister Street, look too real, and I will not sit next to them because they are definitely going to come alive and make fatal bites on my ankles. I feel as though I am the Prisoner of Zenda, who is doomed to die on the rack, while wild dogs howl outside the barred windows. I would leap from the upstairs roof, but for the moat filled with man-eating piranha fish.

I would like to tell Head how the speed is wearing off and about how paranoid I am, but this is impossible, since I know that his advice would be simply to remember that we are all living in mirrors, and that we are all reflections, who must transcend our naïve beliefs in the reality of our negative emotions. I am shaking badly, which is a familiar state of affairs, but this time it could be serious. What if I took too much amphetamine and never come back to normal. I picture myself as a specimen in San Francisco Hospital, the only known case of heart pop.

"Ve haf here, ghentulmenz, a young speed frrreak who vun

day, vile valking in der beatnik area of town, blew into a touzen pieces."

I go into the bathroom and try to put cold water on my head, but my hands are too shaky to turn on the tap. Paralysis. I can't believe it. I am going to be paralyzed for the rest of my days from this. I stare into the mirror and see a blurry image. Blindness too. This is horrible. I will be a hippie basket case, and my friends will feed me brown rice through a tube.

Back in the attic, Mal is looking fantastic (if my eyes are seeing right) in a pair of tight Levi's and a buckskin jacket. She is handing each of the silent people who enter a flower. I try to walk around the other side of the room, because I do not want to let the flower slip through my shaky fingers. Everyone else is in fine spirits. I sit in the back and watch each and every person get into a cross-legged position like yogis.

Head comes over to me, dressed in a fire-engine-red tunic, smiling gently:

"If you will assume the lotus position you will receive the maximum vibrations from the chanting."

I smile and try to pull my left leg over my right one. It will not go. This is horrible. I give a nervous laugh and switch to my right leg. It fits under my left leg, and I smile and try to pull my ankles around. This maneuver causes me unbelievable pain, and I try to lie on my side, to get more pressure on the joints. After several minutes of tugging, I feel my bones snap and know that I have broken my legs. I will be taken to the hospital, where they will beat me with a rubber hose for having long hair. And now, as I lie here on my side, I see Mal take a front-row seat and hear the chanting begin. I try to chant with them but the pain in my legs makes it impossible for me to feel the vibrations. Head is sitting in the very front, rolling his head like a gentle cloud, and I am here in the back in a rare state of horror. I try to nudge up to the guy in front of me to tell him to get me a stretcher, but it's a futile attempt. I do manage to roll over a little, but my feet hit something and knock it over. This terrifies me, and I fear all the hippies coming out of their love trances, under the illusion that I am the destructive force in the room.

What am I going to do? I ask myself.

The pain has moved up my legs now and I am feeling it vibrate all over my chest and shoulders. I am seeing double, and the *Hare Krishnas* are getting louder and louder, and what's more, the pain in my legs is working, *really working*, on my glands and I begin to pee all over myself. I roll to my left and knock something else over. This is no good, and I decide that perhaps this too, this very pain I am suffering, is preordained, that it is a test to see if I am really able to sweat for Krishna Consciousness. So I decide to chant and bear my cross.

"*Hare Krishna, Hare Krishna,*" I say weakly, and then feel a scorching pain at my feet.

"*Hare Krishna, Hare Krishna, Hare Krishna,*" I go on.

Now the pain at my feet is getting hotter, and I jerk my head around and see flames. It appears that I have kicked over a candle, and the flame has caught onto a poster of Jimi Hendrix.

"*Help,*" I yell. "*Help, fire.*"

My voice cannot be heard over the now tumultuous roar of *Hare Krishna, Hare Krishna.*

I nudge up to someone's back and bite it hard.

"*Whaaaaaa,*" the person yells, jumping to his feet.

"*Fire, fire,*" he shouts, grabbing the ecstatic boy next to him.

Then everyone is leaping up and running out. No one is staying to fight the fire. I am still trapped in the lotus position, both legs broken, and the flames licking hotter and hotter. I see Head standing by the attic steps. He is looking past me, at the burning wall.

"Head," I whimper. "Head, help."

"Groovy," he says, "Beautiful . . ."

"Head . . .whoa, *Headdddddd* . . ."

But Head is gone, and I realize that I will soon be suffering from the illusion that I am a piece of smoldering flesh. I begin to roll frantically toward the steps, yelling "Mal . . . Head," crushing the stranded flowers as I go. When I reach the top, I grab the rail and give myself a big pushoff. Then I am rolling, head over broken legs, down the winding staircase. Halfway down, I see Head coming toward me. Ah, I think, he has not forsaken his hippie brother.

"Head," I say calmly. "Here I come, Head."

"Groovy," he says, stepping over my body. "You keep right on rolling, baby. I gotta go back for my stash."

I bite my wrist and roll the rest of the way down the steps.

XXXV.
Back on the Street and My TV Debut

After having my legs fixed at the Haight-Ashbury Free Medical Clinic (they were not broken but merely sprained), I do not go back to the Greta Garbo. I do not want to see Phantom's leering, mocking smile, and the mere thought of Mal's mystical pep talk gives me the shudders. I do not know where I want to go, nor what I want to do, so naturally I end up back on the street. But the street has changed overnight. Now there are ten thousand people, twice as many shops, and all of it is *loud and in living color.* Great swirls of color on little feet marching through the wetness, and underneath the color is a pale, yellow skin, and the bony, protruding jaws which come from the bad food we are eating and the crummy drugs we are ingesting. I stand in the street once again, waving my *Oracle,* which will, of course, run Head's column on this week's method of transcendence. (Maybe it'll be breathing exercises, or maybe it'll be hopping a freighter to Japan, you see what you do is hide in the big cone-shaped things on deck and when you get in there you see Bob Hope and Bing Crosby and the whole thing is a fucking movie and you are back on the street again, high on Methedrine, Methedrine which is *bad bad bad* for you, ask any of the rock bands, it's bad, they will tell you that it is pure death, absolute denial of the living spirit inside, and they will shoot their own arms full of it, and get up there on the *big stage*, and tell you again, for three dollars and fifty cents a head.)

"Bitter, bitter, bitter," snarls Warren.

I do not answer but grind my teeth. Up until this moment, I have not been one to look back, but now I am looking back. It is all I can do.

You might wonder how it is possible to reflect, with those colors swirling by you, and with the speed rushing through you, and the chicks that you are laying, thirteen, fourteen, fifteen, sixteen, balling every night, in someone's strange room, while records are playing, and your friends, your newest friends, are sitting on the other side by the picture of Buddha, shooting more of that good stuff into their veins. But I do reflect. I think of things that I have not told you about before, that I have not thought about until that moment on the garbage street, when there seems to be no future in looking ahead. (And perhaps this is what Head was talking about all along— street therapy.) But I am remembering Kirk, I am remembering Walter, and how they seemed to be living people with certain definitions to them, certain characteristics that you could count on. I think of Walter as gentle, and poetic, and in touch with himself, and I remember him in high school losing that definition as he tried to get into the fraternity. Those wonderful fraternities which were the next step up from the Aces. I remember him carrying books for a boy named Tom Pearson, a boy who is now in West Point. The name of the fraternity is Alpha Pi, and the people in it all looked like Tom Pearson. All of them well built, and all of them walking with their hands at their sides, which was something that was somehow considered "cool." And I can see Walter, walking alongside Tom Pearson, both of them with their hands at their sides like zombies. And in the cafeteria he would carry Tom Pearson's tray, and to show his gratitude Tom Pearson might smash mashed potatoes in Walter's eager face. I remember Kirk telling Walter to stop it, but he was convinced that this was the means to salvation, that only Tom Pearson and Alpha Pi (and the automobiles, and the button-down shirts, and the real silk ties, and the real shell cordovan shoes) could give him whatever it was he needed. So he went on with it, carrying higher and higher stacks of books, and listening to Tom Pearson telling him in front of hundreds of people at the drugstore that he was Walter the goat, that the goat was the lowest form of life on earth, and Walter standing there in front of Kirk and all the others, saying "Yes, I am Walter the goat," and then someone might slip up behind Walter, kneel down, and Tom Pearson would push Walter over the other brother, and, of course, all the books would fall into the street. Kirk and myself would want to leave then, because we would not want Walter to know we had seen him, still smiling, pick up each and every book, all the loose papers in the gutter. Finally, there came the last vote. Walter came to my house, laughing, and wearing his silk ties and his cordovan shoes, and told Freda and Glenn that he was "getting in," that all the things he had gone through were only tests, and that he was finally making it. And I remember Glenn saying to him "That's great." But when I left the room for a minute, Freda came to me and said that she certainly hoped Walter got in, but that she did not trust Tom Pearson because his mother was a snob at the Waverly Methodist Church. And perhaps what I remember

206

most clearly now, standing here on this surreal street, is my own reaction. I am filled with disgust and envy. I want Walter to be blackballed but I am not certain whether it is to maintain his liberty as an individual or anything else. For if he does get in, he will have a big car, and he will screw (or at least neck with) the girls who live in Ruxton, and he will have some strange repellent-charismatic power over me and Kirk. But perhaps not over Kirk. Kirk has thought it was a bunch of shit from the beginning, and is off with Baba Looie in some drive-in hamburger joint, taking some speed (but it is nothing to what is burning me up now). Then, of course, there is the phone call, and Walter has not made it. And he stands quivering on his cordovan wing-tip soles, and the phone is falling from his hands, and he smiles very sincerely at me and says, "I've got to go." I want to comfort him. I am the strong and true friend. "They are just Wasp assholes anyway, Walter," I say, and he nods at me, and goes off in his freshly washed car, and does not come back for three days.

Why do I now begin to think of these old images? It is like a drunk that I once experienced, while trying to look into Susan's window, to catch even one pink glimmer of her fresh-bread thighs. I can see her—yes—she is in the light in her slip —yes—and the slip is coming over her head—yes—and I am drinking sloe gin, without a mixer because I have overheard Aces saying that mixtures are for fairies, and she is standing there in her bra and panties—more sloe gin, and I am sticking my tongue in the bottle imagining that it is Susan's cunt—I have the biggest erection in the world, but then as she starts to take off her bra, I begin to remember seeing Mother Freda and Glenn fucking—it was on a Sunday, and the electric fan had pulled a nice breeze into the house—their bedroom door is open—great hanky legs, little bony acne Glenn fucking—in-out in-out, and I am holding my ragged teddy bear (I chew on

207

it in my sleep, and sometimes wake up screaming, because I am certain I will gag to death, like the small child on "Medic," with Richard Boone, before he was Paladin, and he had acne too, but his acne made people say he looked manly, while Glenn's strawberry skin made him only freakish)—here I am watching Susan, sitting in the bushes, watching Susan, whom I have had my balls busted for, but I have this mental image of Freda and Glenn, and the net result is a feeling of heat, and then of throwing up, all down the bush, all down my khakis— and yes, Susan is naked now, in front of the window, but I am swirling around, Glenn's little white penis, disappearing into this huge dark hairy cave, which no bear would ever sleep in, no matter how cold, no matter how tired. . . .

I wonder why I am remembering this shit. Why are these images floating through my mind with such intensity, the intensity of the clouds Walter and I pointed at up on the Hill so long ago. It occurs to me that then I was free. There on the Hill, digging, I was free. I try to remember other times that I felt like that, but I cannot. Perhaps one or two moments playing touch football, when I would gather in a long toss from Kirk, maybe then I felt like that.

"Get your *Oracle*," I yell. "Get your *Oracle*."

I am aware that I am being very sentimental, and have a great loathing for my indulgent emotions. But the images come forth anyway. I am amazed that I cannot control them. I see myself in the fourth grade, having a hallucination in class— seeing gray dots get larger. I walk up to the teacher, Miss Rochelle, a woman who has spider arms, and I tell her that I must go to the bathroom. She says, "No . . . this is not possible." I insist that I go to the bathroom. I tell her that I must wash off the gray dots, which are now no longer dots but living organisms that are threatening to eat my skin. She looks at me funny, and I pick up the inkwell from her desk and attempt to smash her with it. I miss her, drop the well and walk slowly from the class in a trance. The gray is all over me.

Now I am unable to sell my papers. The idea has come into my mind that I am crazy. This is not whacky wonderful crazy that we all laugh at. This is crazy crazy where you will stand in a white room for days on end. This is not black humor. This is black like the West Virginia night. I am standing on the psychedelic street, shaking badly. More thoughts are going through my head, and mothers are coming by in cars, looking at me and thinking how lucky I am to be free. This is irony. And more thoughts, the worst thought of all, worse than anything I have told you up to now, don't be mad, O reader! Don't be mad! I know I set you up with jokes, this was necessary, this was entirely necessary. Here is the *worst thought of all that was had by me on the street corner of Cole and Haight during the day my mind went all funny:*

I am over at the baseball field, and Walter and Kirk are shagging my feeble flies. After the game, we always play a game called Three Flies In. I hit a long pop, which Walter misses. Kirk laughs at him, and Walter says, "You should blow me, shithead," and then Kirk says, "God will punish you for that." And Walter says, "God? God blows too." Can you imagine my pain, good reader? (And do not let me put you off with dialect, with rhetoric. This is the only honest passage in the novel.) I stood there in the slanting sunlight, in front of the twisted-up backstop, and the words bounced around in my mind. And after the words came images. I had a terrible vision of Jesus Christ kneeling down in front of a huge cartoon cock. It is perhaps important that you realize that the cock was not real, but a definite cartoon, with lined-in folds of skin and charcoal pubic hair. I stood there, the bat dragging in the dust, nearly got smashed by Kirk's throw in, and the picture got animated. Jesus' mouth fell open, and the cock began to harden,

209

which made it go straight up, and Jesus could not reach it. It was way above him. So he climbed on a steel ladder, and grabbed the cock, and went hand over hand (just as we did in gym class) up to the top of the cock, and I stood there right through Kirk and Walter yelling "Hey, Ward, let's go on with the game," as I watched Jesus getting trapped in some pubic jungle, fight his way out with his little sharp, religious teeth, and sit on the very head of it. "Ward," they yelled, but at this time a remarkable part of the dream came into being. Lo and behold, Jesus' mouth had gotten very big and he was sucking on the cock. The image was very real, and I laughed and laughed, and called in Kirk and Walter to tell them. We all thought it highly amusing, can you believe that? We all saw the same wonderful picture. But what happened after dinner was not wonderful. I could not get Jesus and that cock out of my mind. Glenn and Freda would sneer at me over the frozen carrots, and the cock would not go away. The Town of Thatched Rooves was no help either. No help at all. The cock and sick Jesus, and an audio part too, which went "God blows. God blows. God blows" over and over again, some Reed Hadley monotone, simply obscured all the goings on of the Town. And then came the *sick moment of revelation:* I was being made to think of the cock by Jesus himself, as punishment for my own sin. No matter what happened to me from here on in, no matter if I became Johnny Unitas' successor, I would have to see the picture and hear the words. And oh, pure horror! The horror of knowing that what I was doing was all theater, like the Phantom's theater. All of it just a stage show, but I was the actor who would suffer the part. And for six months I walked through the wavy street with Jesus gnawing away on the big cock, and my nights were filled with a glowing, sweating pain in which I begged the Great Master, the Big Fisherman, for some mercy. I also reneged my doings with the Aces (I could not tell this to you one year ago, when I started this, but now I must), swore never to miss church, fell on my knees in frenzied hysteria vowing to go to Africa and become a missionary. No go.

Then one day—and it happened just this way so you must believe it—it all went away. I awoke without thinking of the cock. I went to school and put my hand up Darlene Street's crotch. No cock. No Reed Hadley voice, no nothing. I came home and sniffed glue. No cock. And that night as I sat in the bathtub I remembered that I was supposed to be suffering, and the absurdity of it was too intense for me to believe it. I was tempted to look up into the sky and do a dramatic "Screw you," but I did not wish to press my luck. No cock is all I can tell you. And it went away. For good.

These images rushing through me, and now there is the heaviest realization of all. *I am fucked up.* The thought comes to me like a big blow of air running inside my head. *Bobby Ward, who has seen all the absurdity in this world, fucked up. I, Bobby Ward, like pain. I, Bobby Ward, am just a hanger-on who is trying to be seventeen different things at once and as a result can be nothing.*

My body instantly feels lighter. My head is really a cloud with only impressions for eyes. I am alive, and nobody but me. I do not need to hang on. I do not need to feel guilt, be someone else, find a community, become a mystic. I need to be me. The wonder of the idea makes me want to act like Gene Kelly in *An American in Paris.* I will go skipping down the street, and I will enlist everyone who happens to be watching . . . *No, wait!* That is exactly what I will not do. I will not enlist people. I will not try to be something else. I will be the *real me.* I will go to a house in the country and commune with only me. I will find out just who it is I am and I will be absolutely delighted, never feel guilt; never, never belong to any groups, never, just be me me me. Yeah, that's it.

I kiss myself all over. Tourists roll down windows and snap my picture. I do not see them. I am free, free, free.

Oh, but the elation is also false. The moment of knowing is false, is nothing more than an invention, a bit of logic that sticks to the wall like dried-out tape for one or two seconds, and then falls, like an old scab, revealing the cracks in the flowery paper. Because I am standing here on Haight Street remembering more than I have cared to remember, I am feeling now as if someone were passing a sheet of Pittsburgh plate glass directly through the center of my body.

"Something bad is happening," I say to Warren.

"You are cracking. I have seen it from the start. You are cracking, at the age of nineteen. It will be unpleasant."

I begin to walk slowly away from the thousands of colors, down toward the Panhandle, feeling that plate glass sticking through my body, oh yes. Feeling the body severing like some hard peach, the red fiber in the middle ripping apart, old adhesive from old Band-Aid. "Emotionally Disturbed" will be the sign. A man named Dr. Lou will put me in a room with a black box.

"This is connected to your head, Bobby. You will scream when the depression comes on, but the box will take care of it."

"Yes, Dr. Lou," I will say. But I will feel nothing. I will rock back and forth, like a chair, actually part of a chair. My legs will become maple. Eyes, knots in trees. No, not trees; trees are alive. My eyes will become knots in a chair, dead, varnished trees. It seems to me I have been hiding something. There is a need to recover what I have lost. Other patients in the hospital:

212

A man who offers to trade me a power lawn mower for my cock. He will be hunched over, have a small head and wear a baseball cap and alligator shoes. His name will be Old Charles. I refuse, walk away from this nasty. *Big red nasty.* I would like a bit of remembrance there. I would like the picturesque teacher, but that is not what I get. I am Pensy. I have moved from my seat. My skin is Pensy skin, old yellow the color of musty corners in 1938 living rooms, a big wooden radio sitting under the pool of light. Pensy-me reading the paper. Pensy-me seeing the nighttime slipping away, knowing that tomorrow forty screaming, howling children with revolution on no-minds will march into the world, his-my world. I am Pensy. The patient will sell me one lawn mower and one Feldstar watch guaranteed two weeks for my cock. All this happening to me, boy laugh riot. I tell the patient that he must understand about my condition, that I indeed have no cock, that in my crotch now is a Clark bar, a Hershey with almonds, a Pay Day salted nut roll. I am Pensy. You cannot buy my flesh. The flesh is gone, Mother Freda. The body is gone.

"Warren," I say, attempting to keep up the life-saving monologue.

"Yes," says Warren, in a voice like Pensy.

"Don't play games, Warren," I say, entering the Panhandle.

"Games," says a voice.

Now I am on television. A man with a flat face and a button-down collar is thrusting a microphone into my mouth. He is saying that I will be on tonight's news, that he wants to know my name, my original home.

"I am Pensy," I say, a hardness coming over my spirit, my soul being calcified right here in front of a nation.

"Are you a hippie, Pensy?"

I look at the ground for a body, for a colored leg all black and crumbly. I wait for the Phantom to come and rescue me from this.

"I am suffering from hallucination," I say.

"Then you are a hippie." The announcer is laughing a puppet laugh. I suddenly know that he has gotten that laugh from watching all the other announcers. He is one part of the Announcer, the Big Announcer. It reminds me of *Invasion of the Body Snatchers*, people being reproduced with pods, all their emotions gone, fall asleep for one second and you are hollowed out like the center of the Thanksgiving turkey. Stuffings of you on every plate, every relative eating little bits, all the townsfolk eating little bits, you sitting hunched and stuffingless.

"I am having depression of a serious order," I tell the announcer.

"He means his head is in a bad spot," says a voice. It is the little hippie with Old Shep hair.

The announcer does not like this. He asks me if I am a Digger. No, I am not a Digger, this is a recording, this the disembodied voice doing the recording. No, I am not a Digger, yes, I am for love. Yes-I-am-one-who-believes-that-we-are-a-holy—generation——

Now the little cameraman circles around me. The announcer is asking what we hope to accomplish here. I am answering funny stuff, putting him on. I am saying that I am in Haight-Ashbury because (fill in the ridiculous and colorful answer). I am a member of the Flower Generation because (fill in the ridiculous answer). I hate the establishment because (fill in the answer of indignation). My answers are getting wilder, the crowd of hippies (my brothers, my generation, and *they are*—they are in spite of anything else I may tell you, for do you see any alternatives?) all crowding around me, saying "Yes, I am a smile, I am a groove. Yes, my answers are

214

surreal." For example, he asks me if I am taking care of my body and I answer Yes, both my kneecaps have turned to smiles. "Wow," from the audience. He asks me if free love is not dangerous to the emotional stability of a sixteen-year-old girl. You can see him setting me up, and I take full advantage —I want only to keep this going—so I do not remember that I have absolutely, somehow, turned to dust. This and a fuck and a good shot of something will tell me that I am still here. The interview goes on, I am brilliant. The street is filled with brothers. Do I dream this as well as the mental hospital? Do I dream of America watching me all night, forgoing sleep to sit in ghost rooms seeing me, hearing me, here in the park?

I walk away, dead.

I walk away knowing I am enjoying feeling dead.

I want to kill myself.

I am playing with wanting to kill myself.

I am nothing.

I am corny in my agony.

XXXVI.
In Which the Narrator Crawls Inside the Box

The Phantom is walking in circles around me. He is baring his teeth and clapping his hands. I feel as though he wishes to execute me, and am grateful to him for it. The way I figure it, if Phantom can shit on me enough, I may feel like punching him out, which would be an emotion, and adequate proof that Bobby Ward has not floated away down Lollipop Street.

"So you feel bad?" asks Phantom.

"Yeah . . . no . . . not bad, just gone. Like I am not here."

"So you really feel bad, huh?"

Phantom is playing this for all the drama he can squeeze out of it. If I were here I would find it incredibly juvenile, but I have taken a trip somewhere, if you find me call me and let me know.

"Hey," says Phantom, smacking his hands on my shoulders.

"I just got an idea. If you feel bad, all you gotta do is take more acid and it'll all be different. You'll transcend . . . and everything will be cool. You *need to take a whole lot more acid.*"

"Mockery will get you nowhere," I say lifelessly.

I go over to Mal's mattress and sit down with my hands on my knees. I look at my hands, and keep looking at them. I have this feeling that if I stare at my body too much it will disappear, but I stare anyway, delighting in my own horror.

"Hey," says Phantom, sitting down next to me and taking my hand. "You are a soft middle-class punk who is just discovering that it's all a bunch of shit, baby. Now you got what you came for. Except you didn't think it would mean any difference in you. Right?"

"Of course you are right," I say. "I've been over that already in my own head. I wanted to be something different since I couldn't be me. Now I am going through classic psychosis. You are absolutely correct. I know all the fucking reasons. I can sit here and list them for you, but the fact remains—I've disappeared."

It is at that moment the Phantom slugs me. It's an incredible wallop, and it sends me back on my shoulders, my feet over my head and stuck against the wall.

"Thanks for trying," I say. "Ironic that you would try to make me feel myself with a Zen trick. I thought you were down on mysticism."

Phantom does not give up. He is on top of me, slugging my face and laughing at me, and when I begin to show signs of fighting back he is suddenly kissing me; hugging me.

I want to feel love for him. Maybe if I had not suffered this sudden vegetable state I would actually hold him and weep, and know that I am not dead. But for some reason that does not happen. It all seems like a humanistic Phantom trick. I am disgusted with myself for thinking this, but I say it anyway:

"It's all cartoon, Phantom. Cartoons and clichés. It's a lousy fucking bunch of clichés, the whole fucking mess of it. I've tried it all, you see, and it's nowhere, and I'm nowhere, and this is nowhere, you see. You are another cliché, the tough guy with a heart of gold, and any moment I expect you'll break my fucking neck trying to snap me out of whatever's happening to me, but you can't 'cause there is no me to snap out. I done gone down the fucking drain."

"You self-indulgent little fucker," says Phantom. "I'm not trying to snap you out of anything. I just wanna beat your middle-class slumming ass. You come out here and don't get your babbling paradise, and you have a nervous breakdown. You weak, pimping son of a bitch . . ."

Then, as I expected, he is off me and saying things like I'm not worth the trouble, and he's heading for the door. And just like in the movies, I call him back when he reaches the door and let him make his next speech. But it's a better one than I expected.

"You get your shit together, baby, because you got to catch a plane out of here at seven."

"What?"

"Here," he says.

He throws me a note that he picked up for me at the Haight-Ashbury Switchboard. It says *"Bobby Ward: Please come back to Baltimore immediately. You must report to the draft board October 27. Love, Freda."*

I sit there trying to imagine how I should react. There should be shock and, I suppose, even dismay or a vicious ironic laugh. But I do none of these. I just sit there, across the room from the blank-faced Phantom, very aware that my arms are the reason for my hands, very aware that my feet are the ends of my legs, totally immersed in the beat of my heart.

At the airport I start to shake. Mal holds one arm, Phantom the other. I am having images all over the place, and I am talking a mile a minute to Mal, to Phantom, to the TWA man who will prepare my ticket. I am telling Mal and Phantom all about how I am in this mental hospital, a very funny riff. You should hear me do all the voices:

"Sure, I'm in this hospital, and the doctor is Ed Begley, some old character actor like that. Do you see, Phantom?"

"Get your fucking ticket, man."

Mal looks at me. "Bobby, you really do have to get it."

"Yeah, so I'm in the hospital, do you see? And the doctor is standing over me, right? And he's saying something like: 'Two hundred thousand hours of this man's life, the most formative years of this man's life—years that can never be recaptured—have been spent in front of the television set.' "

People are floating by us now; literally floating by.

"Do you see that Phantom floating?"

The whole place is made of metal, and the lights are neon. If you pop neon a shower of light dust comes out, and it could get on me and eat my skin. I fear neon.

"So I am lying there, Phantom, and the guy is going on about how television fucked me up. I mean, don't you think that's a riot?"

I stop and pull away from Phantom and Mal. I stand in a little open space, watching the people coming and going. I am going to pull a few heartstrings.

" 'Doctor, I have watched, without technical assistance and in a variety of homes—most notably down Kirk's cellar—the following television shows with delight (that is, I'm not sorry) and in a state of complete hypnosis: "Howdy Doody" with

Chief Thunderthud; Princess Summerfall Winterspring—and I cried when she got run over for real, so to speak, on her honeymoon; Mr. Bluster; his good cousin from South America, Don Jose Bluster; Flub-a-dub, Poison Zoomack and . . .'

" 'Wrong,' says the steel arm holding the Tom Corbett laser over my temple. 'Poison Zoomack was on another show dating from 1954, a show with the title . . .'

" ' "Rootie Kazootie" ' . . . See, Phantom, I tell the guy 'Rootie Kazootie.' I know the show. It was this other show, came on on Saturday mornings—not weekdays—and it never had the class of 'Howdy Doody,' and you watched it with a kind of guilt feeling because you felt like you were betraying Howdy and that bugged you for you were never sure that Howdy wasn't going to come right out of the tube and get you with an electric drill."

And now a terrifying guilt comes over me. I have betrayed Howdy. I am Howdy, and I am betrayed, and the strings have been snipped, maybe by Kukla, Fran and Ollie. They always looked so nice but you can never tell, and suddenly I am not a human wreck standing in the airport telling desperate comic memory riffs, but actually in the room I have described, and I know that the room is in the Town of Thatched Rooves, but somewhere some little shred of me is saying "You are not in the Town of Thatched Rooves, you are in the airport," but it is very hard to hear that voice, very hard. . . .

Very hard because the scientists are astounded at my total recall, which is absolutely nothing, for everyone in my generation shares it. We are all image banks but my own are exploding, and you must remember you're in the airport. . . .

"Where are you, Phantom?" I say, holding out my hands like a blind man; realizing what perfect pathos I am creating.

"Here. I'm here."

"I watched 'em all, folks. I watched Johnny Mack Brown,

and the Three Musketeers, Bob Livingstone, and Duncan Reynaldo, and some guy with a dummy name of Elmer who used to throw his voice and got them out of trouble, once Smart threw his voice, and once I thought I was Elmer, right now if you must know, and I watched Red Ryder, are you with me folks, and thought I was Little Beaver and covered myself with red paint, but Freda said it would get into my pores, am I in the airport folks? And once it gets in the pores it will drip over every important organ, and the body which is like a clean, spanking linen closet, but can turn moldy and dusty and you will fall over with your eyes still open dead, how about a little hand?"

"Phantom, we have got to get him out of here."

"No, continue, Robert."

"You're there?"

For now I really don't know. I am looking at Phantom and seeing him opaque, glossy, shimmering, like spray.

"I watched all the space shows, even when I knew they were fake, because you were positive that people in outer space would have to have more on than T-shirts with SPACE PATROL written across the front, but I never complained, never once about it, I loved it all, loved them all, Tom Corbett, Buzz Corey, Rocky Jones, Space Ranger. . . . I didn't gripe even when the rocket ships looked like little fishes moving against a cardboard backdrop, no, I went with it all the way, sitting and eating my Kraft caramels all day Saturday morning, and I dug the 'Sealtest Big Top,' which always featured some trapeze artists who had worked all their lives to thrill me by hanging from a rope with their teeth, and they did it, and I wasn't thrilled but I didn't write in, I didn't go down with a firebomb and try to do in the Big Top, you know I didn't . . . and after that came Winky Dink with a couple two stage, no class, cartoon puppets and a quizmaster cat who looked

221

like he had a square head, and hated kids, and the magic screen for three bucks was a crummy piece of green plastic but I didn't suggest we rip out Winky's intestines, not once. . . . Are you out there, America?"

And I can see Mal, and she is crying and leaning on Phantom, oh good to see it, and for a second I try to tell myself that I am really in control of this monologue, that I am doing it to get sympathy, but then it's all shaking again, the picture is all horizontal lines, weird sound waves. . . .

"Continue, Robert."

"And I watched Beany and Cecil, and all the game shows, even 'Queen for a Day,' and 'Strike It Rich,' and I never suggested we take the Queen for a Day out into some old weed-filled lot and shoot her about a million times, I been a good citizen. . . . Yes, I watched every fake show you sent my way because it was like an electric current through me, do you see, it was like the rock group with the bass booming through your veins, every cartoon you could lay onto my skull, over and over, I swear it, how about that, America? I watched the dancing piggies on Farmer Alfalfa's porch, and the one where the bad *black* dog held up the train station, and kept telling the depot agent to stick 'em up, and when he did, his pants would fall down, and the crook, who had warts on his nose, would say, 'Pull 'em up,' and it went on that way for a long time, years actually, 'Stick 'em up,' 'Pull 'em up,' 'Stick 'em up,' 'Pull 'em up,' 'Stick 'em up,' 'Pull 'em up,' and I never missed a rerun, never missed a commercial, not one in all those years, yes, I watched 'em all, every one, because it made me feel like I was into something, and it made me feel I knew something, and you shouldn't want to fuck with me, because I am an American. . . ."

"Can you remember any more?" says Phantom, jelly in front of me.

I don't say anything, and they are both helping me to the place where we are to sit down, and then it all comes into focus.

"I'm O.K."

"We'll wait it out with you."

"O.K."

We sit in three plastic chairs, staring out the windows, Mal on one side of me, Phantom on the other.

"I was raving, wasn't I?"

Neither of them answers me, and we keep staring out the big windows at the plane. Everything feels like steel.

XXXVII.
On the Plane

On the plane, I receive a voice. It is metallic, the voice of an announcer at the Colt games, and it is my friend. I am sure it is my friend because it is telling me I have got to hang on. So I do. I hold on to the armrest of the seat, and I take huge breaths, and in my head is a picture of Don Larsen when he pitched the perfect game, and he tells everyone in the clouded, stinking clubhouse that he takes deep breaths before every pitch, and I take deep breaths and tell myself that there is a way not to collapse. I will look at everyone in the plane, and I will watch their every feature, and I will not collapse into the seething kettle of images which lies boiling and waiting for me inside my wrecked head.

"Use the eyes," I say to myself. "Use only the eyes. Just see it and record it and don't try to assimilate it."

And for a few seconds it works. An old man next to me. I stare at his skin—brown. He has been on the beach. I stare at his wrists—hairy. He plays golf. I see his silver hair, and his pigskin briefcase, from which the creature hands are taking a portfolio. He is into stocks. And behind this is something in my head. It's as if I am split directly down the middle. For I know that while I am recording these things there is something being built in my brain. I can shut my eyes and see something like nails, and black paint.

Look at someone else.

And I stare at the stewardess, and try not to think of her as plastic. I try not to think of her at all, but simply to record her. To see the eyes, which are blue, and the dress, which is bluer, and the pillbox hat, and the teeth, which are capped. Whiteness of the teeth, and behind my eyes Brain is making sounds. Nails are being driven in, and I know it's the Town of Thatched Rooves, only this time I am not running there to escape from Glenn and Freda, no, this time the Town is coming to get me, to take me away from the legs of the stewardess, which I must stare at, don't think of any metaphors for them, don't see images, just look at those legs, and the whack whack whack in the back of the head, and Brain is making images, and I start to mumble things about Brain. I think that I will make up a Brain poem, and by getting down what I am thinking, defeat Brain, stop it from that whacking, it's a good thing to create art. Pull a pencil out of my pocket and write down the Brain poem; on the back of an airplane magazine called *Wonder Flight*, now isn't that ironic, because now, you see, I do not want flight, is that irony? Now I want to look at the man in front of me is paying one dollar for a little bottle *stop—write a Brain poem on the back of this magazine.*

Perhaps it is a matter of the Brain. The Brain inside the skin, bone, vessels, keeps working. I would like to

225

see Brain pulsate. I would like to see the forehead so profound. The face is a coherent unit making me real. I would like the Brain to show me its act.

I would ask Brain a thousand questions.

I would ask Brain why, when my pants are pushed above my hips, I can feel Walter's red nose move across my face.

I would ask Brain why my arrogant voice is so like Kirk's.

Or if when the red nose and the arrogant voice appear simultaneously I should change my name to Kirker.

Or if I should smell a flower like Mal.

Or if I should remain calm or become terrified when I melt into the sides of cars.

I would like to ask Brain if it can laugh, having no mouth.

These questions are important. These are scathing questions.

I would like Brain to run through them with me.

Now I feel Brain lying in the network of girders, trying to come out through the ear.

Now I feel Brain becoming part of a tree.

Now I relax. My hands are limbs.

I would like Brain to make up its mind.

I would like Brain to come around to my way of thinking.

I sit staring at the page, and sign my name to the poem. I think about sticking it into the bag of the lady who is sitting one seat away. I scan her face, certain that she is a doctor, certain that she has been planted on this plane, positive that she can hear the chopping behind me. I rip the page out and roll it into a ball. It's crinkly in the hand, you can feel it, and you know that it is not a "ball" at all, but only crunched edges. Don't think like that. Look at things.

Look out the window at the clouds, and don't pay any attention whatsoever to the red, flaming image in the head, the grandstand which is being built whackwhack, don't watch yourself up there on the black platform, wearing an ancient waistcoat, high above the beloved townsfolk. Yes, they are craving me, they are craving me and the warmth of the sun, but there is no sun. The sun refuses to set. Blackness surrounds us, only the flickering torches allow me to see them, their leathery faces open in pain and confusion. There is no time for indecision.

I breathe into the shotgun microphones, speaking like an old bug, to my panic Town:

"There shall be sun, O children of Thatched Rooves. There shall be sun and golden harvest. You need not doubt it. Don't give in to self-indulgent fears."

As I speak, there is an illumination over my shoulder, a radiance larger than all the radiances imagined by all the people on any religious holiday you would care to mention. I turn slowly, big-tooth leer cracking my face, my tuxedo tails swishing majestically over the black boards.

"Did I not proclaim it? . . . Observe, my friends . . . observe the fiery orb."

Most embarrassing . . . most . . . 'tis the moon. Not the sun, blessed healer, but cold cold moon. Lord, Lord, one fails to see the humor. . . .

There is a negative reaction to this failure, negative indeed. I am moving slowly along the shadow line, feeling the moon eating out my Brain. In my hand is a one-way ticket to Acrabar, where I shall live out my life in luxurious but sterile

227

banishment. The crowd moves toward me, their mouths moving without sounds, their eyes humming no satisfactions.

"Ah dear friends," I say, backpedaling steadily.

"Sweet citizens," I cry, bowing from my slim waist, the old vaudeville trouper never run out on a show.

A flaming snowball knocks off my top hat. I trip, stumble, indeed do fall into the river, the cold waters gushing into my eyes, nose and lying mouth.

"A drink, sir? Do you want a drink?"

My eyes are on the waitress and she is transformed into an angel. I want to fall on my knees in front of her, go onto television doing testimonials for the flight gals of TWA.

"I could have drowned," I say to her.

"Do you want a drink? Coke?"

"They had me," I say, and then I am telling her that I need a Scotch, and she is saying that will be one dollar, and I am handing her one dollar, but I cannot let it go.

"My fingers . . ."

"One dollar, sir."

And the man with the briefcase is staring at me, but the fingers will not let go of that dollar.

"Take it," I command her. "It's a war injury."

And she is prying it loose, and there are eyes looking at me but it causes little embarrassment, for I am not here to look at, but somewhere running through the gabled houses of the Town of Thatched Rooves, taking big long strides, and gasoline and oil are rolling down the road right toward me, and Fernando Roush is up there lighting it. And I am the cartoon who will not be put all back together again in the next scene, but if you just hold on to your drink, tight with both hands, and keep looking at things, keep staring at them, holding it tight with both hands . . . Yes. Oh, yes. Now that's it. Tight. Tight. Tight.

XXXVIII.
Back Home: Kirk and Walter's Basement

I am standing in the dimly lit hallway at Kirk and Walter's basement apartment.

"Hey," I say, "isn't anyone here? It's me. I let myself in."

No answer.

There are steps ahead of me, steps which lead down to a dark room. I should go on into the room, lie down and get myself together. Perhaps Kirk and Walter are out getting some food or doing a drug deal. But I cannot get up the energy to make my feet move forward. My shaking legs would rather turn me around, move me toward the door. But where would I go from there? Back to Glenn and Freda's, the return of the Prodigal Son?

"Gosh, folks, I was a fool. Forgive me for my juvenile arrogance."

No. Eating humble pie would never do.

I hear a noise from the black room.

I must identify myself.

"Hey," I yell, "it's me."

More noise. Footsteps moving toward me.

"Who is it?" says a familiar voice; I can't place it. Now I really want to run. I turn my body around like a toy robot.

The light goes out.

There is high, hysterical laughter. I must be in the wrong apartment. They will plug me, carry my body to the morgue. PROWLER SHOT BY WIDOW.

The lights go on. I blink my eyes, rub my chin.

"Don't shoot," I say. "I didn't mean . . ."

"Ward. Oh wowwwwww, you're back."

I squint, see her, rub my eyes again. It's no illusion. In front of me is Susan.

"Susan," I say.

She stands there staring at me. I do likewise. This can't be happening. Her blond hair is brown. Her false eyelashes are not false. Her Ship 'n Shore blouse is a T-shirt, dyed with swirls of green, blue and red. She has on paint-splotched Levi's and no shoes. Her toenails aren't polished, and they aren't cut. Where is her Peter Pan collar?

"Ward," she says with a nasal voice. "It's really you."

Now she is skipping across the room, throwing her arms around me. She never did that before.

"Too much," she whispers, hanging off my neck.

"Kirk and Walter are out hustling some food. We just got the stamps from the Welfare Department today. Beautiful scene. Here, come with me."

Speechless, I follow her down the steps. She turns on a wall light, and we are in a big, brick-walled basement with glowing red rugs, some old couches with blue and orange burlap covers. From the ceiling hangs a ball lamp with a red paper shade. She walks across the room and turns on a sterco. The Jefferson Airplane.

She pivots around on one foot, faces me again. Her smile is radiant, beatific. There are many yellow teeth.

"Wow, too much, you're back. I've been thinking about you, I mean, like what I was going to say to you. . . . Whatsa matter? You look like you've seen a ghost."

"Yeah, welll . . . I mean, I'm a little shocked, I guess."

She lights a cigarette and throws her hair around in time to the music.

"Yeah, man, I guess we both are a little up-tight. I mean, man, I've been through some pretty heavy changes since you split, pretty heavy. . . ."

She brushes her hair out of her eyes, takes a seat cross-legged on the floor.

"Like I was totally distraught when you split, you dig? I went over Kirk and Walter's old place and like cried myself sick. Then they began to turn me on to some things, grass, acid, man, and like I went through this incredible reevaluation scene, you dig?"

I nod my head and sit down on the couch. Above me is a poster. It's Trotsky.

"So like then I moved in with them. I mean, man, I just realized why you had to leave and what was happening to me, and like I knew I was repressed. Really repressed. Very heavy. It was really hard not to hate you, man, but I didn't. . . . I mean, after I got my head together; and, wow, things started coming together when I got my head in shape, you dig? So like we moved down here in the ghetto and really started getting it all together, like we ball together and eat together and take dope together and it's a very tight scene. But I always knew you'd come back. And I am glad you came to-

231

night while they are out, so we can groove together on what's been happening. Wow, when you were my old man, I was like sooooooo straight, and, wow, I don't know how you stood being around with me as long as you did. . . ."

This is happening. This is Susan whom I got Bumjarred for, and this is Susan who couldn't stop yawning, and I am not real at all, but an assortment of nuts and bolts, and I got to get somewhere and get a blowtorch and see if I can weld myself a suit of armor. I can wear it around until it grafts itself onto my shrinking and connects up to my ruptured heart. What am I saying to myself? This is Susan?

"You dig this place, man?"

I look around. Our old bookshelf filled with paperbacks. I can see some kind of psychedelic manual and a book by the Head. Lenin and Mick Jagger look down on me from the other wall.

"I did most of this place myself, man," says Susan, rubbing her thighs.

"Like I wanted the place to be loose, free, kind of like an environment. You dig?"

I feel my stomach turning. I see her laughing.

"Look," I say, "I'm pretty wasted. You got a john around here? I got to take a shit."

That was the Phantom talking. It wasn't me. I heard the Phantom moving in on me, saw his long, striding feet walk right into the voice control box and broadcast that to Susan.

She is smiling again, leading me to the bathroom.

"Too much," she says, offering me a joint.

I take a drag off it and give it back to her.

"Too much," she says again, pointing to the toilet.

"What?"

"I mean it's too much, you saying you 'got to take a shit.'"

She knows. She knows that wasn't me talking. She's going to tell everybody.

"I mean like, man, when you and I were married, you would have never said, 'I got to take a shit,' but now I think it's really cool that you wouldn't have any hang-ups about saying it. Like we are really communicating on a whole different level, like we were two different people. There's no past at all. Too much."

She hugs me again. She's gotten stronger. I push her away, enter the bathroom and shut the door. I put my ear to the door to see if she goes away, but she's still talking.

"Hey, man," she says loudly, "like go ahead, take your time. Wow, there's so much time. We can talk about it all. Kirk and Walter will flip to see you. Just relax in there. There's a book on the john to read if you want to. I always read when I'm in there. It's like good for the metabolic system, you dig? Wow, had some boss speed tonight before you came, straight meth crystal. Really nice. If you had gotten here a little sooner you could have done up with me."

I try to twist the lock on the door, but it's broken. I rub my hands together. They are not my hands. I look into the dusty mirror. My face is all lean, weird looking.

"Hey," she says again. "Like you in the bathroom reminds me of your old man. Does he still spend all that time in there? Weird. We've gotten stoned down here a lot of times and had many smiles about him. What a freak."

I am staring at myself, and the stomach is turning turning, and I am seeing Glenn's face in that mirror. Hiding. Hiding in here, trying to get away from Freda and from me, with my insane juvenile raps, and it's Glenn putting that acne cream on himself, and then it's my face back again. Hiding in here. Speed freak Freda outside the door. Oh Christ, I am sorry,

233

Glenn. I didn't realize what was going on. Go home, tell him how sorry you are. All that comes out is Phantom's voice. All that comes out.

I sit down on the toilet, shaking. She's out there, Susan, Freda, Baba Looie, Phantom, Taco Lily, Howard Zucker, Japanese grocer. I am back home, I am straining to get it out. My old man is cutting it all out. This is sickening. I am straining, straining, feeling sick about Glenn, throwing up about Freda. Poor poor Freda and mad slashed Glenn. What will happen? I am straining. What will I do? I'll get it all out, that's what I'll do. I'll strain and strain until I project myself right off this toilet seat, right off it, you hear. Yeah, and I'll go spinning across Baltimore right on this seat, spinning and spinning like mad; and I will land at Kirk's house and rap on the door, still sitting there on the seat, you gonna see it. When his mother opens the door, she will think I have come to shock her, to "gross her out," as the college boys say; but I will take her tenderly by the hand, sit her down in her living room and tell her that I am sorry about Kirk.

"Is there anything I can do?" I will say.

"What on earth do you mean?" she will retort.

"About Kirk I can do nothing," I will say. "It is an accident, a genetic freak. I am terribly sorry, though. I want you to know that I, Bobby Ward, sitting right here on this toilet seat, do sympathize with you. I am sorry. Really. I am sorry Kirk takes drugs. I wish it wasn't so. I am sorry he wants to overthrow the government. He's right, but I am sorry. I know that back there in 1945 when you had this baby, all pink and cuddly, you had no idea it would turn out like this. Admit it, it'll make you feel better."

"It's true," she sobs, holding my free hand. (With the other I am wiping like mad, but it keeps oozing forth.)

234

"Oh, you are so right," she says. "You pierce the very heart of the matter. If you only knew what I've been through with that boy. And now, Kirk's younger brother, Robbie. It's the same with him. No respect. None at all. He calls us pigs."

"With Robbie too, huh?" I say, biting my lip.

She begins to cry.

I join her.

"Listen," I say, all choked up. "I know a lot of kids who would appreciate a nice home. Good kids. Orphans, actually. I could send them over here for an interview. You know, pick one, two, any number you want."

"No," she moans. "It's just not the same. A mother loves her own."

"Give the orphans a chance," I say, falling on my knees at her feet.

There is a long silence, and then she moans louder. I see that there is nothing anyone can do.

"Good-bye," I say, hugging Kirk's mother. "I'll go see Walter's folks now."

"Yes," she says, forcing a brave smile. "Maybe they could use an orphan."

I walk around the corner to Walter's house.

His mother comes to the door. She sees me, all ragged and defeated, sitting on my toilet seat. A big vein pulsates in her head.

"Come in," she says. "You'll be arrested for sure."

"I just came to tell you how sorry I am it didn't work out," I say.

"What's happening to everything?" she cries, handing me the tissues.

"I'll do anything to help," I say. "Anything in my power."

"What power?" she says.

235

"*Too much,*" yells Susan. "*Totally different level.*"

I go home to my parents. Glenn greets me at the door with a scalpel.

"I see it all different now," I say.

I am led into the dining room. Freda is bouncing her black potatoes off the wall. I rush into her arms and console her with kisses. If I could get this turd out it would be all different. If there were some air currents in here I could breathe again.

Susan is tapping tapping tapping on the wall again. Keeping time to the Jefferson Airplane. I am straining, crying, gagging. I pick up the paperback on the toilet bowl. *Revolution* is plastered across the front.

"You drowning in there?" says Susan.

"I got to take a piss," says Warren. "Hurry up in there."

If I stay in here. If I never leave here. If I do like Glenn do, jes stay in here all de time nevah come out, they call fo' me I tell them nobody home, jes de cleanin' man in here, ain't nobody home tall. If I stay in here forever and ever, and don't fall off this flying seat, this wingding zoomin' airtravelin' seat, if I don't fall off because all the king's horses and all the king's men ain't never gonna let me get my shit together again.

I let rip with a long fart, pull down my pants and watch it fall, all liquid out of me. I want to put it back in. I should get Susan in here to stuff it back in.

I sit on the john here. I ain't flying nowhere. I got no place to go.

XXXIX.
Meet Me at the Bottom

But lo and behold, just when you think you have hit rock solid bottom someone comes along to show you where the real floor is. Such a person is Faye, Walter's new girl. Short, compact, with red-brown hair chopped close to her head, big green eyes and a wide, wide mouth. She walks into the cellar and sits down with Kirk, Susan and myself. Right away I am worried. She has that look, that look I recognize only too well. It is the look of a person with power, with her own vision of things, and I am afraid she will somehow influence me. It sounds absurd, but since my near collapse after San Francisco, I am wary of anyone with any magic. But it's no use. Immediately, she changes my life, and how I despise her for it.

What happens is as follows. She begins to talk, stoned disconnected from the hash, but eventually the talk somehow comes around to her father. He is dead, but before he died he had been a carpenter, a Swedish immigrant who came to

New York in the 1930s. He worked for "the pigs" all his life.

"But he never gave in, man. He was always organizing, you know? Always. They threw him into jail in Newark. They threw my mother into jail with him, for wearing pants and smoking a cigar, and yet neither one of them stopped organizing. They were beaten a hundred ways, but the one thing they gave me. The most valuable thing."

I look around the room. It is late. Kirk has fallen out over the hookah. Susan is asleep on the rug. Only Walter and myself are still awake, caught in the spell of this ugly, beautiful girl, and I am afraid. Very afraid. She has awakened something in me and I don't like the wave of nausea I am having.

"What did they give you?" I say.

Faye stands. I see her in the bad light, short, frail, but incredibly strong. Next to her I feel insubstantial, flimsy and superficial. I think of the Phantom, of the Stumps. What did I really see there?

"What they gave me was a belief in man. A belief in myself. They never were beaten because they never once . . . not once . . . identified with their oppressors. They didn't tell me, 'If you don't please the teacher, you are bad.' Instead they told me that I may have to do what the teacher tells me, but I must realize that he is wrong, that he is often oppressing me. It was great for me. I loved my parents, and I have a hard time understanding people who make buffoons out of theirs."

Now she is staring directly at me. How could she have known? Then I remember. This whole conversation got started because I was entertaining my friends by telling the "Glenn in the bathroom" stories. How I hate her for bringing this up.

"You didn't live with me," I say. "You don't know what it was like with my folks. They were the exact opposite of yours."

She is stalking back and forth across the room now, her

238

plaid cape trailing behind her, casting a long shadow, like some horrible vampire that will suck out the truth. I wish she would disappear. I want to meet nothing but bland people. I don't want to be pushed anymore. I feel sick for mocking my folks. Suddenly the words "my father" come into my head, and I feel faint. For now, right now, with this total stranger pacing the floor, I feel the painful humanity Glenn possesses. It's almost magical. For the first time in my life I understand that Glenn is a person, just like myself, with his own feelings, thoughts and misery. It's a feeling I guess you are supposed to have somewhere around eight or nine but I have never felt until now. And with that come grave terrible doubts. How much have I shut out? How much have I killed off other people in fear, in vanity?

"You and your fucking stories," I say to Faye.

"What?" says Walter. He is drinking some wine. I walk over to him and pick up the bottle. I am shaking all over.

"I am sick of your fucking stories," I say.

"I'm sorry," she says. "I didn't mean to attack you. But if you get into certain political things you can't allow easy satires like yours to go unchallenged."

"What?" I say. I can't hear her right. I can't see her right. Everything is trembling.

"What has politics got to do with anything?"

"A lot," she says, "if you understand the dialectic. . . ."

"What is that?" I interrupt. "A fucking disease? Help me, doc, I got the dialectic."

Walter is standing up with me. He is trying to hold me back. I must be swaying. I know he is only trying to help, but I am so ashamed of myself, so washed through with guilt, that I push him away.

"Listen," I say, "I don't need to hear any of your political riffs. You unnerstan'? I been through the whole boat ride of

239

fucking answers. I been a Ace, a Stump, a con man, a saint, and I been fucked over all the time. So do not lay any of your Marxist ass views on me."

I am slumped on the couch, my stomach sticking through my sweat-stained T-shirt. Susan is lying at my feet with her mouth open. I am Bobby Ward, and I seen it all. I had high hopes and now I am just like my old man, except worse. Both of us in the bathroom, two snakes of the toilet, sitting there shedding skins for the American Television Hour.

I stand up.

"Ladies and gentlemen," I say. "I, Bobby Ward, will now shed the first skin for you. First, the inner self. Shed and discarded at age seven. After that is gone all the rest are by necessity mere hallucinations and aberrations. Fake skins. Colored nice, lovely patterns, but they crumble at the first touch. . . ."

I am waving the wine bottle high above my head, drowning in self-pity, amazed at my own disintegration. I who had such lofty ideals. But then, I know that's a lie too. I haven't had any ideals. Just wanted to find a good skin that I could wrap up in, be safe in. Now they are trying to sell me another new one—the radical skin. Dare to struggle. Dare to skin . . .

"Bobby," Faye is saying, "I understand you. I know where you are at. I've been in jail, and nearly lost my head, but the one thing you must understand is that you are good. That it's the pig who has put you through these gyrations. Do you think any healthy society would have people going to the lengths you have just to find themselves? You have to understand that what's happening to you is happening to all of us, and if you want it to stop you have to understand the forces that have formed you. . . ."

I am thinking of my old man. I see him there in that bathroom. I think of me in the bedroom, turning it into a TV play so I can deal with it. It's a cartoon. You can deal with a fucking cartoon. But what happens to a mind that reduces reality to a cartoon? Where does the body go? Who owns the heart?

"I do not want to hear any more of your shit," I say, pushing Walter.

"You need help," says Faye. She is moving toward me. I know her game. They will get me soft so they can use me in the revolution. Or am I reducing them to a cartoon so I can handle them? Where am I? Who *is* on first?

"What's on second," I say.

"Help me get him to bed," says Walter.

"Fuck the dialectic," I say. "Faye, I know you. You are the little girl in the fourth grade, the one who cries because she only fucking got a ninety-three on her report card."

I am enraged at them. How I want to smash them. Their dialectic. Their working class. My father. My cartoon. Help a man into the bed, but please master Marx, don't you spill the wine.

XL.
Walter Is Not My Friend

Walter is not my friend. He and Faye are out to hurt me. With these absurd ideas ingrained in my paranoid head, I take up with Kirk and Susan. They do not like Walter and Faye either, so the three of us smoke grass, drop acid and listen to records all day. We talk a lot about our "freedom." Here's Kirk:

"Like Walter and Faye are always talking about the Movement and how you can be free through politics, uhhh, ummmm, ah, fucking roach burn my finger . . . cough cough gag."

Susan: "Yeah, and like they don't understand about freedom. I mean, like we are free right now. Really free. Whereas they jes think they are free, the assholes. . . . Anybody wanna screw?"

Me (feeling very profound after thirteen Dexamyls, fifty joints, some nice coke and an acid tab): "The whole freedom thing is a question that can't be answered unless you are into the not-self, because freedom is not freedom to consume, but freedom from personality, and the not-self is all bound up with the dwarf self inside the leg o' mutton goat blip of the future. . . . What the fuck you doing, Susan, get offa ma joint."

Kirk: "Cop my joint awhile, Sue baby. Hey, man, that not-self rap was pretty heavy . . . I mean, very heaaaaavy."

I listen and participate in all this idiocy, and when I have taken enough drugs it almost sounds real. Soon as I crash, however, and the head caves in like some old mine in a 1936 Western, and the fuse to the dynamite is burning burning burning and little Bobby Ward, hippie dope freak, is racing to put it out, and he covers it the last minute because he is sure that it's a grenade but hey ho, what you know? it ain't no grenade but a fuse after all, and it's blowing up up up, the top of the head coming right off, kind of like a cliff of brown charred dirt with a rug of green slime moss on top, and it's all blowing up again again into the blue smog sky. And I am sailing along through the air, Stump Family playing, and here I am rapping this complete nonsense, and Faye is absolutely right, I don't know shit about Hegel or Marx or anything else, so why am I presuming to judge her, who does know, and you know Bobby Ward, as sure as the amphetamine crash leg pain in your ass is coming on, that you don't like to give that Faye no credit because she is a woman, and you do stand condemned an adolescent who ain't so young, an intellectual what thrown away his brain, a revolutionary fast turning old and fat, and worse, oh worse, a male chauvinist pig of the high hump order. You is bad.

And I am, oh friends, sitting alone in my ghost room, the drugs swirling in my burned-out singed good brain, and there come Faye and Walter down the street, not wasted, not defeated, not mouthing clichés, and oh how I would love to race down there and have them explain the diarrheafuckinglectic to me one more time. But do I dare? Ah no, because I am still trying hard hard hard to be a saint, still looking crystal vision into the Town of Thatched Rooves where all is dead, quiet and dull, and Fernando Roush is no longer a villain of any note, no longer the threat that makes the legs arms heart pump fearful but good life. Nah, he is nothing. Runs the movie projector and shows nothing but home movies. Here is one of his flying tapir pigs, but then you seen it all before, what say, Warren? Seen it all before.

"You are truly reduced to bathos," says Warren.

"Yes," I say, "tired and gray and old and only twenty-three years of age."

Yes, it's damn sad. Most unfortunate. I am on a sinking ship called Self, the U.S.S. Self, and I am too fucking tired to swim, and too embarrassed to call Help to another captain. And there before me, like a beacon of all I hate, but still am, is the big SEARS sign pumping useless evil vibrations of purple blue energy out into the polluted capitalist Baltimore death-ray sky.

"Poetic," says Warren. "Poetic."

And now I am opening the window, though I feel like a fool, and the cold cold air is whipping in over my face, and hands, and Faye and Walter are looking up at me from the street.

"You wait a fucking minute there," I say. "I'll be right down."